Eleven Stories

and More

Kressmann Taylor

Copyright 2016 by C. Douglas Taylor

CONTENTS

2016 Introduction ………………………………… 5

The Blown Rose…………………………………… 9

Take a Carriage, Madam …………………………. 33

The Red Slayer……………………………………. 39

Passing Bell ………………………………………. 51

Mr. Pan …………………………………………… 66

Goat Song …………………………………………73

Girl in a Blue Rayon Dress ………………………. 82

The Pale Green Fishes……………………………. 93

The Midas Tree ………………………………….. 121

First Love ………………………………………... 154

Michael …………………………………………... 166

Notes on 6 Stories……………………………….... 181

The Controversy Poems………………………….. 183

More Poems………………………………………. 201

Appendix: Kathrine Kressmann Taylor Chronology….. 215

End Notes……..………………………………….. 217

2016 Introduction

by C. Douglas Taylor, son of Kathrine Kressmann Taylor

Kathrine "Kressmann Taylor" Rood, (1903 - 1996), "the woman who jolted America" in 1939, was born in Portland, Oregon and later lived in California; New York; Pennsylvania (where for twenty years she was a professor at Gettysburg College); Minneapolis, Minnesota; Florence; and San Casciano, Val de Pesa, Italy. Her story *Address Unknown* was a national sensation in 1938-39, and since 1995 has been republished in America and England, and in twenty-two other languages world-wide.

Kathrine Kressmann Taylor also wrote an additional eleven stories, all included in this volume, and three other books, *Until that Day,* 1942, an account of a real-life struggle against the Nazi takeover of the German Lutheran Church, *Diary of Florence in Flood*, 1967, (titled *Ordeal by Water* in England), and *Storm on the Rock*, 1978, a novel set in post-war Italy, published to date only in French as *Jour D'Orage*, in 2008.

Most of Kathrine's short stories were written while she was busily occupied with other endeavors: She wrote *Address Unknown* and several of the poems in this volume while living on as small farm in Oregon, where she ran a household without running water, raised three small children, gardened, cleaned, and cooked while her husband Elliott worked in San Francisco as a magazine editor, usually home only on weekends. After the publication and great success of *Address Unknown* she was able to move to Nyack, New York, hire household help with the children, now four in number, and write a full-length book, *Until That Day*, 1942, reissued in 2003 as *Day of No Return*, (in German, *Bis zu Yenem Tag, 2002*).

When "Address Unknown" was published in *Story* in September, 1938, and followed with a hardcover book version printed by Simon & Schuster in 1939, it allowed her for the first time the freedom to stay home and write. In 1942, with the proceeds from *Address Unknown* Elliott and Kathrine bought another farm, in Pennsylvania, near Gettysburg, where, because of her literary reputation, Kathrine was soon offered a guest lectureship at Gettysburg College, a small Lutheran-related liberal arts college. Her first course, Creative Writing, attracted such student interest that she was offered a full-time instructorship after the first year, and she continued to teach there for nineteen years, becoming the first woman ever granted professorial status, and the first ever granted tenure.

Life on the farm allowed little time for writing, nor did life as a full-time professor. The farming was turned over to a neighbor in 1949, thus freeing the summer months when the college was not in session. From 1949 onward there were mostly just the two of us, my mother and I, in the household, except for my two-year absence to serve in the army, and I got to know her daily routine fairly well. During the academic year she concentrated solely on her teaching, and in the summers she wrote short stories, partly because of the limited vacation time, and partly because the short story was her favorite and most successful format.

As I recall, her favorite time for writing was at night, perhaps because of the quiet, perhaps because that was when inspiration came most readily. She wrote at her portable Smith-Corona typewriter, usually with a cup of coffee at her side, and she indulged herself by using only the finest china cups, her English *Wicker Lane* Spode, and always a fresh cup, never a reuse. I recall waking in the mornings to find her asleep in bed and six or seven used cups and saucers scattered on the kitchen table.

She never discussed what she was writing until she thought the story finished. Then she would announce to her colleagues at the college that she had a new story and they were invited to the farm for a reading. They always came *en masse*, and she would read the story aloud, quite dramatically, and to instant and quite vocal approval. Usually this reading would be my own first experience of the new story.

After my father died in 1953, my mother continued for thirteen years teaching at Gettysburg College and writing short stories during the summer vacations. At the college, Kathrine was a very successful and admired teacher of creative writing, journalism, and Literary Foundations, an inter-disciplinary course in which she took great interest and initiative. She even took a sabbatical leave and went to Florence, Italy to do research on Dante for the improvement of the course. She was much admired by both students and colleagues, and for years her considerable energies were directed more to teaching than writing. Finally, when she retired in 1966, she could devote her energies to full-time writing. To facilitate this plan, she decided to move to Italy, where she could live more economically on her small pension.

Here fate took a hand in her plans. On her voyage to Italy on the Italian Line's *Michelangelo*, she met the American sculptor John Rood, a widower, who was to become her second husband a year later. The two had a shipboard romance, and with plans for marriage in the future, she settled in Florence, in a pensione on the bank of the Arno River. It was there that she witnessed the great flood of the Arno in 1966 and the ensuing recovery of the city. Most foreigners fled the city at this point, but she stayed on, writing an account of the international rescue efforts to save the city and its art treasures. Her account became her third book, *Diary of Florence in Flood*, (*Ordeal by Water* in England) published to great critical acclaim the next year.

Following her marriage to John Rood, Kathrine put aside her writing for the next seven years, and only after his death in 1974 resumed writing with her final book, a novel, *Storm on the Rock*, which she finished in 1978. In her last years she began a reminiscence of her early days in Oregon, which she entitled "That Other Eden," but she only completed twenty or so pages and left it unfinished at her death, late in her 93rd year, in 1996.

She never wrote another short story.

THE BLOWN ROSE (1)

"For thence, --a paradox
Which comforts while it mocks, --
Shall life succeed in that it seems to fail."

-- Browning: Rabbi Ben Ezra

It was five o'clock and the shadows were turning blue in the long living room. Alice Arnold wondered uneasily whether she might not set a match to the fire that waited, neatly stacked, the sticks laid crosswise like a child's log house behind the shining brass of the andirons; it was only that Mrs. Tevis was still puttering around with a dust cloth in her hand, lifting, so very delicately, the Dresden cups on the mantel, half touching them with the soft cloth and replacing them with a diffident precision, stepping back with her head cocked to regard their placing -- like a thin, tiny plucked hen, Alice thought--then giving a confident nod, moving slowly in her thick, horrible old boots across the room to the bronze elephant on Robert's smoking stand and giving it just the least brush, a tender, brief twitch of the cloth in her quaking old hand.

She's been at it all afternoon, Alice thought, and her eyes explored the corners of the room where, surely, the floors had not been waxed, not even dusted. Why on earth hadn't Maud warned her? But her eyes, as she followed Mrs. Tevis's vagrant progress with the dust cloth, held more of perplexity than of irritation. I'm paying her for a full day, she said in her mind, and was surprised to discover, as her glance ran over the half-done room, that the thought held more affection--yes, it was really almost affection--than annoyance.

When Maud had heard that their efficient Lydia had been called away for two weeks to tend a sick sister, she had thought a moment and then said briskly, "Of course you can always get Mrs. Tevis. She does need the work, poor lamb. And she's a darling, really, in spite. . ."

The "in spite" should have warned her, Alice thought, but

Lydia had already been away for three days and the house was in a state; so Mrs. Tevis had come. The door chime had announced her at nine, just after Robert had left for the office, and Alice had found herself totally unprepared for this tiny swathed bundle of a woman, whose clothing seemed rather wrapped around her in layers than put on her properly, whose ankle-length dresses--surely there were at least three dangling hems each a few inches below the next – these dresses were still not long enough to hide the huge boots, a sort of cracked rubber galosh with broken metal clamps on the insteps, which encased her feet. She had not taken off the boots all day, and she walked with such an inching shuffle that Alice had begun to wonder whether she had shoes under them. Preposterous, of course, but it would hardly have surprised her.

But Mrs. Tevis's face did not permit pity. Mrs. Tevis was gracious. Her prim sweet little mouth with its cultivated British speech; her pallid eyes, kindly and vague but with a sort of familiar desperation in the way they ran over and over everything in the room, over Alice's face, hardly resting on it; the looping folds of desiccated flesh that sagged from the clean skeleton-thin chin bone; her tiny twisted hands showing the brown splotches of age on their backs--all these were held together by some sort of far-away strength, a faded distinction, the whisper of distant and long-decayed drawing-rooms, which put Alice suddenly in a subservient position.

"Now what may I do for you, Mrs. Arnold?" Mrs. Tevis had asked, after she had unwrapped herself from the outer layers of her nest-like covering; first a shapeless brown raincoat, whose front flap had been folded around to the back and tied to the empty belt-loop on the right with something that might have been a shoelace, then under that a man's tweed jacket out at the elbows. Alice, vaguely troubled, had found herself ushering Mrs. Tevis through the hall and into the kitchen, where, abandoning her plan of having the new help wash the floor first, she had brought out instead the silver drawer, the polish and the polishing cloths.

"May I sit here?" Mrs. Tevis had asked, moving a

vague hand toward the breakfast table, where the dishes still sat, and Alice had found herself picking up the littered china hurriedly, clutching a handful of knives, forks and spoons and scooping them out of the way, carrying them to the sink.

"Please don't hurry for me, my dear," Mrs. Tevis had insisted gently, her palms resting, oh so daintily, on her thin knees; and Alice, with her hands full, suddenly felt bubbling up within herself a complication of emotions that was part mirth, part exasperation, and part a slender, almost unacknowledged delight.

"Charming," Mrs. Tevis said gravely, her tiny hand fluttering over the silver. "Such a pretty pattern." She took up a spoon and began to dab over and over at the handle with a smattering of polish. "What a pity," she went on after an interval during which the same spoon had received an almost fairy-like patting-on of polish to the bowl, "what a pity the modern sterling is made so thin. When I was a girl at home, we used to have such beautiful heavy spoons."

Alice, her hands deep in soapsuds at the sink, wondered for a shrinking moment whether the old lady was consciously patronizing her. Not quite, she felt. There's that air about her. She puts me in my place without even trying to. I'm definitely middle-class; it's funny how she can make you feel it when we don't even think of ourselves as middle-class in this country. She glanced at the tilted grey head at the breakfast table, the hair quite thin and rather kittenishly curled around the edges (curling tongs, nothing else would do it) and the serene shrunken face whose puckered skin was hardly more than a shadow over the clear skeleton, the straight, slender nose, the nostrils sunk to flabbiness--the grotesque mat of garments. How funny she is, really, she thought. But Maud was right; she's a lamb, somehow.

The silver polishing went on seemingly without progress, and Mrs. Tevis replaced each burnished piece in its nest with careful solicitousness, her fingers hovering over every completed fork or spoon with a trembling benediction, a little moment of pleasure and release that had to be relished and fulfilled before she went quietly on to the next.

Alice learned during the morning, as she washed the kitchen floor on her knees ("Please now, let me move, dear Mrs. Arnold, so that you may wipe in here. You must not for a moment allow me to be in your way.") a great deal about Mrs. Tevis's past life; or rather, she gathered bits of richness, tiny nosegays of reminiscence, which she endeavored to piece together. Mrs. Tevis must have moved at one time in circles of distinction; great names dropped from her lips with a wistful familiarity that could not merely be designed to impress. They seemed to come softly out of the past and wrap themselves about her absurd old head like a mist in which figures moved, alive.

"We were at dear John's -- Mr. Galsworthy's. It was such a blow to us both, his death." A sigh, while the desiccated hands fluttered over the silver. "That year at Aix we saw Cezanne several times. He looked so old. I'm sure he had no idea he was going to die so soon. He showed me some wonderful things about colors. I was painting then, you see. Although he was often sulky. He said the most lovely thing to me one day. I had wondered about his making so many studies in one spot, and he said: 'you have only to turn your head a bit and it will all come new--*tout devient frais*.' Wasn't that fine? Nevin, my dear husband and I have so often said those words to each other: 'Just turn your head a bit, and it will all come new.'" She smiled, and Alice was surprised at the brightness that lit her peaked face. She took three hours to do the silver.

After lunch, which Alice prepared and her helper consumed with the same considerateness, the same trembling daintiness, Alice turned firm and asked Mrs. Tevis to wash the dishes.

"But, my dear, I should be so happy to. Please let me."

Mrs. Tevis spent an hour absorbed in the froth of the dishpan, delicately swabbing and re-swabbing every plate and cup with little tender touches that did not seem quite to bring them clean. Then Alice, gauging the probable timetable of the afternoon, asked her if she would mind cleaning up the living room, and left her with a cluster of mops, dust cloths, polishes, wax, and sweeper, and took the car for a much-needed two hours in town.

When Alice returned just before five, Mrs. Tevis was still at work. Those old boots move as slowly as the years, Alice thought, but her hands hurry; they move so fast, with such trembling haste, and yet she never seems quite to touch any object she comes near. I wonder if she's done a thing.

The doorbell chimed. Mrs. Tevis ceased her perambulations, stood still and smiled.

"That, I believe, will be Mr. Tevis coming to call for me."

She looked calmly at the litter of cleaning utensils which still cluttered the living room. "I wonder, my dear, if you would help me put these things out of sight now? The room is hardly in fit shape to receive a gentleman, is it?"

Her smile was confident, and Alice saw that she was suddenly very happy. Quickly, like conspirators, they carried the cleaning equipment back to its closet.

Alice received Mr. Tevis at the door. He was a tall, surprisingly handsome old man, with ruddy apple cheeks and the candid blue eyes of a child. He wore a trim, very white chin beard, which made him look distinguished, and he was dressed, his tie new, his linen spotless, the collar of his shirt stiffly starched and considerably higher than men were wearing nowadays. His air, for he definitely had an air -- Alice put aside the word "swashbuckling" for the word "courtly," which came nearer, but there was something of both about him. He held her proffered hand and bowed over it.

"So this is little Mrs. Arnold. What a pretty thing you are, my dear."

Without waiting, he turned his head, glancing into the living room where Mrs. Tevis stood waiting, and called in a rich, happy voice:

"Bertie, Bertie, my love, you are here, aren't you? Eh?"

"Won't you come in?" Alice found herself asking.

Mr. Tevis beamed down on her. "A little visit," he cried, and his voice, she noted, was masculine, deep, and totally without guile, "a little call. Charming, charming. Bertie, my dear, a soft chair for you. Yes, yes, a soft chair. You need it. You look tired." He pulled round a padded yellow arm chair, and Mrs. Tevis sat down with a look of quiet pleasure on her face.

"Delightful place you have here," Mr. Tevis declared, stretching out his long legs from his seat on the davenport. Alice saw that his shoes were shabby -- polished, but the heels run down and both soles worn though.

"I was just speaking about you young people last night. With Eli Strohman. You know him, eh?" Eli Strohman was an art collector and connoisseur of first rank in the city, and the young Arnolds (Robert was just getting solidly established with his architectural firm) had no more than a slight acquaintance with him.

"Why, we know him to speak to," Alice said.

Mr. Tevis pulled up his legs and leaned toward her over his high knees, and his voice dropped in tone to intimacy.

"He thinks the world of that young husband of yours, my dear," he said. "He thinks the world of him."

Alice began to feel a slender thread of uneasiness, of suspicion almost, of lines of life a little too fantastic to be quite real, gathering about her. Galsworthy, Cezanne, Strohman – She was disturbed, at that moment, to hear her husband's key in the lock and to have him come in to find her established with the Tevises. The two men shook hands.

"I was just telling your wife," Mr. Tevis said happily, "that I heard something of you two young people last night, from Eli Strohman."

"Is that so?" Robert Arnold said. He shot a quick glance at his wife and saw that her face swiftly pleaded with him, although at the end her eyes twinkled. He grinned back at her. "How about a cocktail, Allie?" he asked, "Don't you think the Tevises might join us?"

"Well now, splendid," Mr. Tevis assented, nodding his

beautiful white head and bringing his palms together in a gesture of approbation. But Mrs. Tevis murmured, almost in a whisper:

"Oh, nothing so strong, please. A little sherry, perhaps? She looked hopefully at Alice. "Dry," she added. Another glance passed between the Arnolds.

Alice was in the kitchen, where she had prepared a plate of canapés, had poured Mrs. Tevis's sherry and was adding a last jigger to the cocktails when she became aware that Mrs. Tevis had followed her. The little spotted hands were quivering again, and Mrs. Tevis murmured, "I wonder--" Alice waited, the cocktail shaker icy in her fingers.

Mrs. Tevis's mouth had gone slack, but she composed it. "My dear, she said firmly, I wonder if I may ask you a great favour."

"Well, of course," Alice began, "that is, if it's anything I can--"

"My dear," Mrs. Tevis hesitated. "It's rather difficult, isn't it? You see, it's about my pay."

"Oh, that." Alice exclaimed hastily, a little shocked. "I'm so sorry. Of course I'll give it to you. I didn't mean to neglect it. It's only that the men came in while you were working. Of course I'll pay you."

"I'm afraid you don't quite understand," Mrs. Tevis said. "It's so difficult." Her eyes met Alice's, and behind the composed, ravaged old face, in the pale time-bleached eyes there lay dread, a sickly fear. "It's only," she murmured, "that it would be so much more pleasant, for Mr. Tevis, if you could let me have it when he is not there." Her breath went out of her like the last sigh of steam from an exhausted kettle.

"All right," Alice agreed, somewhat bewildered. "I don't have my purse in the kitchen, but if you like I can take you into my bedroom for something before you go. I didn't mean to forget it."

"You would never have forgotten it, my dear," Mrs. Tevis said gravely. "You are a very charming child." Her hands again began their indecisive flutter, and Alice said quickly:

"Perhaps you'd like to help me. Will you be good enough to take these in?" giving her the plate of canapés. I'm honestly beginning to talk like her, she said to herself, as she followed the shuffling little figure and came into the living room bearing the tray with the shaker and glasses.

Robert had lighted the fire in the fireplace and was leaning back, smoking his pipe and listening to Mr. Tevis. And Mr. Tevis was in his element; his ruddy distinguished face was alive, was animated with pleasure, and his hands, long and very white, waved happily as he talked. He was in Brittany, Alice noted as she passed the glasses. No, suddenly he was in Paris, a Paris long past; but the web he spun was lighter, airier than the little skein of memories drawn out by his wife during the morning. They must have been there surely, but how he was embroidering it! The great names appeared, flickered, were gone -- Monet, -- Degas -- Denis. --a shower of anecdotes, little personal touches as deft and vagrant as the poses of a ballet dancer. Here it was again -- Renoir.

"And Bertie!" he cried suddenly and, turning to his wife, he bowed deferentially. His look of pride made his face very pleasant. "She was quite famous, you know." Mrs. Tevis bowed slightly in return, like a grave little Buddha, and then her husband was off again, to London this time, where the names were literary names, and again the cobweb dome floated.

Alice glanced at her husband. It was all right, he was enjoying it, and she relaxed to enjoy it herself. What a wonderful old humbug the old man was! He really was an amusing story-teller, his voice, that happy voice, dwelling with relish on every detail of that long-past time, bringing them alive: the marble colonnades -- the crowded London streets -- mist on the Thames and the sparred shipping. She knew with a flash of intuition that this was the only adult she had ever encountered who was happy as a child is happy, lost in the present moment, wrapped in his own pleasure. Life must have given him everything he wanted, she thought--everything; and

Eleven Stories ... plus

then she looked again at the Tevises in their shabbiness and thought how absurd that was.

The old man was certainly an amazing raconteur. The Diamond Jubilee, Victoria. That was back in the 1890's, wasn't it? How old are they? I wonder if she's older than he is. Heavens, she looks it, by twenty years, but that's hardly possible. The 1890's, she would have to have been twenty at least--plus fifty; certainly he's over seventy. She picked up the thread of the story again. Really, he has charm. I'm sure he's not consciously faking it. It's his simplicity I like in him, just as I like in her--good heavens, what is it I like in her? It's not easy to define. I like her, though.

Mr. Tevis's narrative had been drawing them by careful, suspenseful steps into the dusty offices of a famous London publisher where a manuscript of Conrad's waited to be read, when he broke off abruptly.

"My dearest Bertie," he cried, his face breaking into a dawn-like smile, "here I have the most famous surprise for you, and I haven't told you."

Mrs. Tevis leaned toward him eagerly, her strange little skull-like face with its flabby dewlap flushing almost like the blush of a girl.

"You haven't found someone, Nevin?"

Mr. Tevis cleared his throat portentously, while his face beamed.

"It's the most extraordinary thing!" He turned confidentially to Robert Arnold. "Extraordinary how things happen to one, isn't it?" I can't get over it." He turned back to his wife. "My dear," he announced, "I have an inside track, an absolute inside track--to Dunn and Harrington."
He held his pleasure back excitedly, waiting for his wife's reaction.

"Oh, my dear," Mrs. Tevis breathed. She lifted her weirdly framed head and closed her eyes, and the look that came over her face was like a prayer of gratitude.

"Dunn and Harrington," Mr. Tevis beamed. "Absolutely the best publishers in the business, wouldn't you say?" he asked

Robert Arnold, then without waiting for a reply, "Yes indeed, yes indeed. They know how to put a book across, those gentlemen! Publicity, you never saw anything like it. Half a million copies is nothing to them."

"But, Nevin, how--?" Mrs. Tevis was eager, breathless.

"Wait until I tell you," Mr. Tevis cried. "The most extraordinary thing. D'you know I've been waiting years for a contact like this," he told the Arnolds. "The inside track! That's what counts, of course. Everybody on the outside has a book to sell. Everybody. Masses of manuscripts--crates full of them. What happens? Your book goes in. Absolute unknown. Manuscript goes to some underling -- back it comes. Publisher never even has a look at it. Some of the finest things in literature batted themselves around publishers' offices for years, positively going begging. Conrad went through it, you know." He sat back, and the firelight reflected itself in little triumphant gleams on his cheekbones, his snowy neat goatee, the points of his collar.

"But let me tell," he said. "I still can't get over it, the way it happened, you know. It was the merest chance, the merest chance." He spoke to Mrs. Tevis: "I just happened to be down around the docks this noon. Wonderful stroll there along the waterfront. And I went into this little lunch counter. Haven't eaten there for months. Don't know what made me go in there today. Fate? We don't know how these things happen. But there I was. And who should sit down on the stool alongside me?" His eyes went over their faces in turn, relishing his moment of suspense. "The man who used to be Ben Harrington's chauffeur!"

Alice was stricken with a shock of dismay. But Mr. Tevis was happily unaware of any incongruity.

"Yes indeed," he said. "Harrington's own chauffeur; knows him well. Known him for years," He turned to Robert. "Perhaps you are acquainted with the way these publishers handle things, Mr. Arnold? Do you know what they do? Get a manuscript they like—seems fine but they're not sure of it?

You probably think they'll show it to some literary critic, get an expert opinion on it? No indeed, not at all. It's the public taste they want. The great public. They'll hand the manuscript to the cook, to the chauffeur. 'Read this. Tell me what you think of it.' The chauffeur comes back in the morning--hasn't been asleep all night. 'Mr. Harrington, I couldn't put it down' Great! That's the book we want. Set the publication date; rush it into print. Yes indeed, yes indeed."

There was complete silence. Alice was afraid to look at Robert. She looked instead at Mrs. Tevis. Mrs. Tevis was bent forward; her rapt face, turned to her husband, was lighted by candid belief, by a wholly naked joy. Alice's heart winced, and she turned her eyes away, stung by a sharp pain, stung--almost by envy.

Robert's voice broke the stillness. "So you have written a book, Mr. Tevis?"

"It is nearing completion, sir, nearing completion. At last. The work of a lifetime. Isn't it, Bertie?" Mrs. Tevis gave him a warm secret smile.

"I wonder if you'd mind." Robert asked, and Alice was again able to look at him and saw that his face was wryly composed, "would you mind telling a couple of outsiders something about it? What sort of book is it? What's it about?"

"A layman's question," Mr. Tevis said indulgently. "No indeed, I don't mind talking about it. It is about. . ." he waited until their attention was almost strained" . . . Man." he said.

"Oh," said Alice.

"And now," said Mr. Tevis, all in a moment pulling himself up onto his feet, "My dear, we must be going. We are keeping these young people from their dinner."

Mrs. Tevis got up, and Alice, remembering, said, "Mrs. Tevis, you'll want to primp a little, comb your hair, wash your hands before you go out." She took the old lady into her bedroom.

Five dollars, Maud had said, was Mrs. Tevis's price. It was considerably lower than the regular scale of pay for day help, and Alice understood the reason, now. Five dollars! She wasn't worth even that. Nevertheless, as she handed Mrs. Tevis the folded bill, it seemed somehow shabby not to give her more. But Mrs. Tevis felt the whole proceeding was perfectly correct.

"I'll see you tomorrow then, my dear?" It was a question. But in spite of the half-cleaned living room, the three hours over the silver, Alice knew there was no possible answer but yes.

At the door Mr. Tevis was expansive. "Delightful," he told them, shaking hands, "thoroughly delightful. If you young people will indulge us, we shall come again. We go out very little. And it's good for Bertie, it's good for Bertie." His eyes, looking down at his wife, were brimming with tenderness, and he tucked her little brown hand into the crook of his arm and laid his thin white hand over it, holding her so, as he led her carefully down the steps.

"Well, what do you know!' Robert said, as the door closed. "That marvelous old fraud! Do you know, I honestly liked him."

"So did I. I thought it was wonderful."

"What an act," Robert chuckled. "He really had me going there for a while. Until he got onto this book of his. Ben Harrington's chauffeur, good God!"

They burst into simultaneous laughter.

"What a mountebank," Robert said, "what a beautiful old mountebank!"

"I think they're both darlings."

"The wife?" said Robert. "Oh, he fades her out completely. She doesn't seem to be much. Just a shriveled little old mouse."

"I don't know," Alice said thoughtfully. "I don't know."

Next morning, however, Alice's liking for Mrs. Tevis suffered a strain. She had given the old lady a vase to clean.

"It's not properly called vase, my dear," Mrs. Tevis

corrected her primly. "Vahz, one should say vahz. It's a pity to hear our English pronunciation corrupted."

Alice felt a quick flare of resentment. She goes too far, she thought. Doesn't she realize how absurd she is, playing the great dame here while she hires out for housework? Then she was ashamed, of the thought and of her irritation.

She set Mrs. Tevis to cleaning the bathroom, and while she herself sorted laundry in the kitchen, she smiled over the fantastic outlines of the Tevises' story. She even began to resent a little Robert's dismissal of Mrs. Tevis as negligible. That humbug of a husband. She began to feel protective toward Mrs. Tevis.

She had to pick up some clean tea towels from the linen closet in the bathroom, and she found Mrs. Tevis touching, dabbing at the bathtub fixtures, oh heavens! patting, frittering. She does need somebody to look out for her.

"Mrs. Tevis," she asked and was frightened by her own boldness, "Do tell me, has your husband ever had any of his writings published?"

Mrs. Tevis received the question graciously. "Oh yes, my dear. Yes indeed. In England before we were married, his essay in the *Quarterly Review* was very well received; it attracted some very favorable comment. Very." She allowed the cleaning to languish and smiled at Alice. "Then, of course, the conception of his great book came to him, and since then he has given his whole life to it."

"He began it in England, then?"

"He began it, yes, but we had just been married, and there were so many distractions. It didn't go well at first. He realized, we both realized, that he must have absolute solitude. And that is when the thought of America came to us. We knew about the wilderness, you see."

"You went into the wilderness?"

"Well, really not too far. There were other considerations. Mr. Tevis felt we should not be too far from New York City, so that he might enhance his small inheritance on the New York Stock Exchange. We realized it would be necessary," Mrs. Tevis confided gravely, "to husband our resources. Even then he could see that the book would be a work of years."

"So, we went into the Catskill Mountains," Mrs. Tevis went on, her sentences beginning to spin themselves out with a smoothness that marks a story that has been told before. "My husband invested a part of his resources in a tract of land there. It was a wooded tract, and from the wood on the property he constructed a house for me -- a cabin, you would call it."

"You mean he built it himself?" asked Alice, incredulous.

"With his own hands," Mrs. Tevis answered proudly. "It was very brave of him. You will realize, of course, that he had never been accustomed to work with his hands. It was quite a large house," she said happily, "with three windows and a door. The flue, the chimney, that is, he forgot at first, but that was added later. And the forest around us was so beautiful."

"The only unfortunate thing," Mrs. Tevis rambled on, and she seemed almost to be talking to herself, "was the roof. You see, he began building it from the top. It seems quite logical doesn't it, to begin building a roof from the top? And of course it seemed so to him. Only you see, the lower rows of wooden tiles had each to overlap the row above them from the outside instead of nesting under them. Do you see how it would be? And of course the rain could not run off. In bad weather it was wet, very wet."

"But how did you manage? cried Alice. "How could you?"

"Oh, we put a waterproof over the bed, dear. And Nevin was brave, very brave. Although I fear we never did quite get used to it. I'm sure it was then that Nevin contracted his throat ailment. But he would never complain."

"But how long did you live there?" asked Alice, appalled.

"Four years," said Mrs. Tevis. Her strange old face wore a glow, and she seemed to expand under the release of these confidences. "Such a happy time! A forest changes so from day to day when you live in it; and Nevin used to read me bits from the book when he had done something especially fine. Oh yes...Yes, we lived there until the blow came, when Nevin lost his money. Men," she said softly, "whom he had trusted completely--he felt they were friends, true friends – advised him very wrongly about his investments. But he has never blamed them, Mrs. Arnold," she said with dignity, "never once. He has a very beautiful nature, my dear." She smiled softly into space.

"And then?" Alice ventured, but she had spoiled the mood of confidence. Mrs. Tevis's look came back to her, quiet, reserved.

"Then it was rather difficult, of course."

"But Mr. Tevis's book? Did he have to abandon it?"

"He would have," Mrs. Tevis replied. "In fact, he insisted on it. But of course that was quite out of the question. Still, it pains him when he has to be aware that I--help out. He has said to me many times, 'Bertie, I refuse to be a burden upon you.' That, of course, was the reason for our little subterfuge yesterday."

"But what did you *do*?" asked Alice, frankly probing.

Mrs. Tevis's long silence reproved her, almost frightened her; then, "Many things," Mrs. Tevis said severely. "For a time I painted children's toys." She shut her lips painfully.

Alice was as shocked at the pain she had given as at the truth revealed by Mrs. Tevis's sudden taciturnity. She sought eagerly to make amends.

"And I suppose," she murmured, when it was hard for you, you had only to turn your head a little and it all came new--"

Mrs. Tevis's face lightened like a child's. "How charming of you to remember that," she whispered. "It really has been like that for us, but so many people are not able to see it." Her smile went wandering off into the clouds and then came back slowly.

"Dear me, my dear," she said, "now what would you

like me to do next? Shall I polish this mirror for you? It does seem a bit spotted."

"Oh yes, please. If you will, please." Alice gathered her tea towels and halted at the door. "Mrs. Tevis," she said, "You know your accent is still very British. How long have you been in this country?"

"Since 1903," Mrs. Tevis told her complacently. "I was thirty-three years old that summer. You see, I did not marry young. Better to wait for the best, my dear."

Alice carried the towels to the kitchen, horrified at the implacability of her arithmetic. "She's eighty," she told herself, shaken, "She's eighty."

Mrs. Tevis continued to take Lydia's place in the household for the next nine days, or, rather, she continued to come to work, and Alice found as many light tasks for her as possible. Mr. Tevis had not again stopped to pay them a visit when he arrived, as he did punctually every night at five, to call for his wife.

"He has more restraint than I gave him credit for," Robert observed.

On Mrs. Tevis's last day with them she came wearing a pair of shoes, new, cheap child's oxfords of brown and white leather. How tiny her feet were! She displayed the shoes to Alice at once, with gentle pride.

"I felt it was quite wrong. I thought Nevin should have the new pair. His are very bad. But he would not hear of it; he insisted they must be for me." Her pale eyes were clouded with pleasure. "He has a very 'giving' nature, my dear."

It developed that the Tevises had even another reason for rescuing "Bertie" from the ignominy of the abandoned boots. They were "going out" that evening. They were, in fact, going to a very elaborate affair. Mr. Eli Strohman was holding a reception at his gallery to honor two great French painters who had just arrived in this country, and there would be a small, intimate party at his home afterward. The Tevises, it appeared, would attend both functions. If the verbose, the

Eleven Stories ... plus

white-and-rosy Mr. Nevin Tevis had told her this, Alice would not have believed it for a moment, but since Mrs. Tevis had revealed it, her credulity wavered all day on the thin edge that separates belief from disbelief. Mrs. Tevis's undisguised joy unquestionably weighted the side of credence.

Late in the afternoon Mrs. Tevis came into the room, hesitated, and then spoke.

"My dear, if you don't too much mind, I should like your opinion on a matter that I'm afraid does disturb me a bit."

Alice waited. She had become almost fond of Mrs. Tevis's wandering circumlocutions.

"You see, it's my dress. I don't know. Do you think this dress will be too dreadfully out of place? I don't wish to be -- noticeable, you know."

The dress, which was certainly the same one she had worn every day for the last nine, was so nondescript that Alice had never looked at it closely. It was a faded cotton, bleached almost white from wear and washing. What shape it might once have possessed was long since gone; the sleeves sagged, and beneath the uneven hem protruded, as always, the bedraggled hems of two other garments. Alice's mind ran frantically over her own wardrobe. The blue velvet -- she had not worn it for three years, and it was too tight for her. But it was pretty well out of style. Would Mrs. Tevis mind that? Her glance ran with wild irony over the alternative. All right, then. If only I can get her to take it.

"It's really not too bad," she said carefully, turning Mrs. Tevis gently by one fragile shoulder. "You always keep your things so clean and fresh. Still, it's not very dressed up." She hesitated. "I have a velvet dress that I can't wear anymore; it's too tight for me. But you're smaller than I am. I've kept it only because I don't like to throw out good clothes. It's of no use to me. If you'd like to try it...?"

"May I see it?" Mrs. Tevis asked, and Alice thought: Good, that's the first hurdle. But she was not prepared for Mrs. Tevis's face when she took the dress out of its tissue wrapping.

Her prim little mouth grew hungry, and her trembling hands fingered and fingered the soft blue fabric.

"Oh no, my dear. No, I couldn't possibly. It's much too beautiful. The color--"

"I do wish you'd want to," Alice said, "especially since I can't get into it. I'd love to give it to you if you'd be willing to take it. I've worn it, you know, so it's not new. Why don't you just slip it on and see how it looks?"

Mrs. Tevis permitted herself to be persuaded, but to Alice's dismay she insisted upon pulling the velvet on over the clothes she was wearing. It was not a bad fit, especially with all that bulk under it, but the velvet had a low neckline, and the washed-out collar of the cotton protruded above it. Alice noted too, with apprehension, that the velvet was just an inch shorter than the highest cotton, so that four laddered hemlines now hung above the bright new shoes. But it was Mrs. Tevis's eyes that hurt her; they were the eyes of a child looking at a Christmas tree. She saw nothing beyond the shine of the velvet. With a hurt in her heart, Alice watched Mrs. Tevis capitulate to her image in the mirror.

"My dear, you are much too good to me."

"It will look still better, said Alice practically, without those other things under it."

Mrs. Tevis shook her head, smiling. "Oh no, my dear. I should chill."

So that was that. Mrs. Tevis rested for the remainder of the afternoon in order not to be tired for the party. They talked very little. Alice's fingers were itching to tuck the cotton collar out of sight, to pull up the few inches of cotton sleeve that hung below the velvet sleeve, but something restrained her. She was afraid of damaging more than she might mend.

Robert met the Tevises at the door as they were getting ready to leave, and heard all about the party. The good-byes were effusive all round. When they had gone, her husband turned to Alice.

"Your dress?"

"I gave it to her. I can't wear it."

"But, good God, she's not going to wear it like that, is she?"

"My dear," said Alice softly. "I'm very much afraid she is."

Robert threw himself on the davenport, laughing.

"What an amusing pair of old idiots! Why, Alice, what the hell is the matter with you?" for his wife was trying to laugh but instead was sobbing shakily, tears running helplessly down her cheeks.

The next evening Robert Arnold came home full of a story to tell his wife.

"What do you know? They do know Strohman."

"I'm glad," Alice said.

Robert Arnold had met Eli Strohman with a group of friends at lunch and had mentioned the Tevises to him.

"That's right; you know them don't you?" Strohman had asked.

"They're friends of yours?"

"Very old friends. They were out at the house last night."

"They told us they were going. Tell me; they seem such an odd pair, such a---" Arnold groped for a word, and Strohman smiled. "How did you ever happen to meet them?"

The older man sobered. "Don't you know who she is?"

"She?"

"That's right. No I don't suppose you'd know her name even if I told it to you. It was so long ago. She was Alberta Nigle. Mean anything to you?"

"I'm afraid not," Arnold admitted.

"She came to Paris," Strohman said slowly, in the early 90's. I've forgotten what year, but it was still in that wonderful flowering period of the Impressionists. Some of them, Pissarro, Cezanne, were already growing old. But what power they had! Renoir--ah, well. And then *she* arrived. Alberta Nigle, an intent, sober little thing. But she had a way of laughing suddenly that was like a splash of yellow oil on a dark palette."

"She was a painter?" Arnold asked, when Strohman did not go on.

"I was nothing but a boy," Strohman said, "sixteen--seventeen. And I thought I was a student, but I had only the love of it, not the hands. But Alberta--she was already good. And how she learned! She could watch one of them at work for half an hour, and know everything. Miraculous! Another twenty years, ten even and she'd have topped them all. I am sure of it."

"Funny you never hear of her."

Strohman pursed his lips. "Hm-m. Well, there were only half a dozen or so of the best canvases, after she found her style. The Metropolitan has two of them. I am fortunate enough to own one."

"I'll be damned," Robert Arnold said. "But what about the husband, the old boy? He seemed to me to be the one--"

"Ah," Strohman's face was urbane, expressionless, "yes. Charming. She's devoted to him, of course."

Lydia returned, and the house was restored to its usual pleasant order. The weeks went by, and they did not see the Tevises again, and gradually the queer old pair faded from their minds. Alice had mused for several days, at first, over Strohman's story. A painter? Was that why the little blotched hands always moved so fast, so gropingly? Yet there was something uncomfortable in the recollection of Mrs. Tevis, and Alice was almost relieved to let the memory of her grow dim.

Three months had passed when, on an evening when Robert was out at a meeting and Alice was alone in the house, the doorbell chimed, and Alice answered it to find Mrs. Tevis standing there, trembling and even more wanly frail than she remembered her.

"Am I disturbing you, my dear?" she asked, and in her voice was a high note of strain which gave Alice the momentary impression that the soft words had sounded shrill.

When she sat down in the living room, her face blanched to such a greenish pallor that Alice hurried to the kitchen, chose a big-cupped Burgundy glass and filled it to the brim with sherry. Mrs. Tevis sipped it twice as Alice held it to her lips, but after she set it down on the small table beside the chair, she did not touch it, and it sat there, a small gleaming bowl of amber in the firelight.

Mrs. Tevis began to chat, about everything, about nothing. Reminiscences of her days with the Arnolds, the weather, her girlhood in England, disjointed scraps without connection, without reason. And underneath the murmuring voice there sounded, somehow, taut as wire, the high terrible whine of strain, of fear. Alice found her heart beating hard.

"Look, Mrs. Tevis," she broke in, "is something wrong?"

The old woman's eyes came slowly out of vagueness into focus. "Thank you, my dear," she whispered, "thank you so much. You make it easier for me. You see," she said unhappily, "I had to walk all the way. I wasn't able to find the bus fare," Her hands began to jerk, spasmodically. "And I went to Maud's first; only the neighbors say she is out of town. And that was all of five miles. And then I came here, hoping--"

And it was a least two miles from Maud's house to theirs. No wonder the poor old body was worn out. "Please take a little more of the sherry," Alice urged.

"No, no, my dear, it would go to my head. . . and you see it's so necessary that Nevin have chicken broth. . . oh dear, I'm not sure what I came to ask you. It's so difficult. He's never been ill before. And of course I can't go out to people and take care of him too, can I? And he must eat, for the sake of his strength. He's so weak it quite frightens me."

"But of course we'll help," Alice said. "Why didn't you tell me at once?"

"It's so very difficult, Mrs. Tevis muttered, "I came to ask you to lend me a dollar. I shall return it at the first possible moment. It will be a sacred obligation--" Her speech was toneless, rehearsed.

"Look," Alice said urgently, "I want you to lie down a little while. You're tired out. Then as soon as my husband comes with the car, we'll drive you home, and we'll leave you money enough and some things your husband can eat."

"No", Mrs. Tevis cried, "oh no, I've been gone too long." There was a frantic urgency in her as if Alice were trying to hold her prisoner. "No, no, I can't. If he should wake up and miss me--"

"All right, Mrs. Tevis," Alice spoke quickly, soothingly. "Please, you may do whatever you want. Only let me put a few things in a basket; you can't shop tonight. And then I'll put you on your bus." She patted the fragile shoulder as she hurried into the kitchen, but as she pored distractedly over the shelves, she was scared -- scared. The old woman's arms were beating, flapping, rattling against the chair arm.

Chicken broth, thank goodness, two cans. And some of that dried-pea soup. Crackers. A quarter of a pound of butter, grapefruit. Why didn't she keep more on hand? She laid a concealing napkin over the contents of the basket and came back with it into the living room.

Mrs. Tevis pulled herself up onto legs that shook like quivering wires, but her face warmed into a gratitude as lovely as sunrise. The beautiful clean lines of the little skull face appeared through the disfiguring flesh, and something as wonderful as glory began to shine through her. She stretched out one hand for the basket, then slowly and tenderly she collapsed at Alice's feet in a heap, like the petals of a blown rose that loosen all at once and drop in a soft mass to the ground.

The Arnolds' doctor was out and could not be reached. The hospital attendants who came with the ambulance were noncommittal. Alice could not endure the thought of the charity ward.

"We'll pay, for a day or two anyway," she said, hoping that Robert would not be annoyed with her. But it turned out

Eleven Stories ... plus

that there was very little to pay. Mrs. Tevis died that night in the hospital. Of exhaustion and malnutrition, the doctor told them. Oh, no.

And no one knew where to find the husband. The Arnolds had never known the Tevis's address. Maud had called Mrs. Tevis for them in the first place, and Maud and her husband were off in the south somewhere on one of their leisurely and unplanned trips with the car. Strohman had gone to London. And no one else knew anything about them. A telephone number? They could never have afforded a telephone. Some rooming house, probably. The police were not greatly concerned to locate a man who was in his own house, not until Alice cried at the captain frantically that the wife had starved to death -- starved to death! Then they began their methodical searching. They found him on the third day, on the top floor back of a decayed rooming house, whose landlady had become uneasy. And he too was dead -- of pneumonia, the police surgeon said. No, there were no signs of undernourishment.

Because Strohman was abroad, the Arnolds took with them the great bulk of manuscript from the old desk. It was hand-written on grey newspaper copy-paper, a large part of it yellowed and crumbling with age. They spent a long time over it, page after page. And there was nothing there. Disconnected jottings, strings of words. . . half paragraphs. . . doodlings. . . tic-tac-toe. . . unfinished sentences. Nothing.

"I can't stand it," Alice told her husband.

"It's too bad, all right," Robert sympathized with her. "But it's probably a good thing they both went." He looked at her for a moment, then picked up the evening paper and settled back in his chair.

Alice looked around her bright familiar living room, so safe, so pleasantly matter-of-fact. So stale and unprofitable, And all at once she saw, like tangible things, the years coming toward her, day after day. She remembered suddenly, vividly, the pain and the glory on old Mrs. Tevis's face, and she wanted to cry out in terrible desolation to her husband, to cling to him.

Kressmann Taylor

But Robert was absorbed in the sports pages.

# #

Take a Carriage, Madam (2)

by "Sarah Bicknell Kennedy"

An Entry in the New Writers' Fiction Contest, 1935

Madam was going up the stairs ahead of me. As I came into the big, dim hall I could see her pulling her heavy frame laboriously up, one slow step at a time, then pausing for breath before she essayed the next. A black-gloved hand clutched the high banister. The other arm was full of bundles. I was tired myself, this evening, and this tortured triumph over each separate step by the huge woman was more than I could endure.

"Can't I take some of your bundles for you? You're overloaded."

Her small black eyes, a moment before dull with effort, snapped at me.

"These young people! How many do you think have passed me every day on the stairs? Do they stop? Do they even say 'Good evening, Madam'?" Her eyes suddenly blurred and the voice swelled to a tearful whine. "No one thinks of an old woman any more. I'm just an old woman and they leave me to get up the stairs alone. Thank you, dear, thank you. You're too sweet. You mustn't tie your happy young steps to my old ones. No, no. I couldn't ask it."

The whine had dashed my small private glow over my generosity in stopping. I dreaded whining old women. But I was in for it. Protesting, I took the greater bulk of the bundles and laid a hand on her elbow. In silence, except for her breathing, we conquered each tread together, paused and encountered the next.

The vast ceiling, a mosaic of red and blue tile, arched above us into the shadows of the second floor. The house had been a great mansion before the San Francisco fire, but was now in its dotage, and the wide, enormously high staircases served morning and evening to try the leg muscles of the roomers. I had seen my companion upon them often. She made daily, laborious pilgrimages outside and back to her room on the second floor. I did not know her name. I don't believe I ever learned it. The landlord spoke of her as "Madam," and so we all addressed her, when as tonight, one of us was not too engrossed in his own small affair to think of it.

It must have taken us ten minutes to surmount the stairs. I carried the bundles into her room. Again her little dark eyes blurred as she caught my arm in an effusion of gratitude.

"Sit down, dear, sit down. I would so like to have you. These young people have lost all sense of courtesy, but you thought of an old woman. I should like to show you some of my things. Perhaps you haven't the time. You have taken so much time already. But I'm sure you'd be interested. Could you stay for ten minutes? I would so much appreciate it. No one calls on me. But you would like to see my things. I have some great treasures here."

Her voice rattled as she walked heavily about the room. It was one of the better rooms of the house, large, with three bay windows and a white tiled fireplace. The table, couch and chairs were littered with little scraps of sewing, feathers, lace and silk.

"You wouldn't believe it, how they used to contend for my creations. One of the best dressmaking houses of Paris. The Countess of P. . . .wouldn't wear anything I hadn't made. One of the very best houses. He used to say, 'Madam, go out on the boulevard, well--no, take a carriage, take a carriage and spend the morning, spend the whole day, but bring me back a costume, one of your creations. Take a carriage. Go!' and I would take a carriage and drive along the boulevards. Then when I came back I would make him a suit, or a gown. He would be wild with joy. 'Take a carriage, Madam,' he would say."

She opened a huge old wardrobe and began to bring out armloads of clothes, silk brocades and heavy, musty broadcloths, coats and dresses in the style of the nineties, with tiny pinched waists and flowing skirts, gorgeous materials, infinitely tucked and frilled and pleated, with braid and fur and feathers in profusion. One by one she held them up before me, the grandeur of forty years ago.

"Aren't they beautiful?" she cried. "Aren't they beautiful? Women don't know how to dress nowadays. Look at this blue broadcloth. Fifteen dollars a yard it was. And the lovely, tiny waists! Would you dream that I had worn this, dear? Yes, in the spring before my second marriage. My husband was so proud of my figure. I could put my two hands around my waist. But now I am an old woman, old, old!" Her enormous form shook with a Rabelaisian sign.

"They were so elegant, the women of fashion then. I had a genius for elegance. He used to tell me I had a genius for elegance. Do you know, dear, he would send me out to spend all morning on the boulevard? 'Take a carriage, Madam,' he used to say."

Her little black eyes gleamed accusingly at me, as if daring me to deny the recital of her triumphs. Then they suddenly watered with tears again.

"There's a little girl, such a sweet child, she works in the bakery shop down on the corner. She is always so good to me. Let me show you something. She doesn't dream it but I am going to surprise her with a wonderful present. Such a sweet, good heart she has, just like yours, dear, with kindness in it for an old woman." She rummaged among the sewing on the table.

"I am making her this. Isn't it lovely?" Upon her hand poised a hat, a floppy, shapeless reproduction of a camper's khaki headgear in brown silk and gold braid, with peaked crown and loose, drooping brim, a horror of a hat. It was fashioned with the most exquisite needlework, and it was fantastically, unbelievably ugly. Madam's wide, wrinkled hand caressed the silk.

"You'll never find goods like this today. This was a dinner gown, but I cut it up. Try it on, dear. It would be beautiful on you. Dear me, you have so much hair, I'm afraid it's too small. But it would be beautiful on you. Do you know what I shall do? I shall make you one, too, when I have finished this. There's a great deal of the material left. I'd like to make you one in appreciation of your sweet, thoughtful heart. Then perhaps if your friends liked it they would order some from me. You won't find anything like it; it's quite unique. Just as soon as I finish this you must come in and let me take your head size.

"Don't go yet, dear. Surely you can spare an old woman another five minutes. So few call on me. I want to show you my dolls." She opened a deep drawer in the wardrobe. "I've been dressing them for months. I have sacrificed some of my dearest treasures to them, but they're worth it, the darlings! Look at this sweet little blonde."

Dolls they were, ten of them, with placid bisque smiles and brown or yellow curls, but the rest of them was obviously of Madam's individual manufacture. Their bodies were long and wasp waisted and their costumes were reproductions in exquisite miniature of the gowns and suits she had been displaying to me a moment before.

"See, dear, I've made them quite perfect, even to their lovely little chemises. And they all have their three pretty petticoats, flannel for warmth, ruffled white for daintiness and silk for elegance. This little blonde is my pet; you'll never see velvet like that today. They're to go to some dear little girls at Christmas time. Don't you think they'd make a little girl very happy? Such an elegant lady to have for her very own?"

Her eyes, all at once, were pleading with me. The fright in them belied her confident sentences. I looked at the little blonde. Her smirking bisque head was an anachronism above her antiquated finery. The plum colored velvet of her gown was musty and stiff as canvas. I knew with a quick certainty just what a modern little girl would think of one of these dolls, but I smothered the judgment in a hasty wave of pity.

"They're perfect, Madam, they're just beautiful. I've never seen such lovely little costumes." I was urgent in my protestations, so much more enthusiastic than I felt that I had a half fear that her pleading eyes would resume their shrewdness and blast me for a liar. But she was in too much need of reassurance.

"Thank you, dear. I'm so glad to have a young girl's opinion. I have spent such hours of work upon them, the little darlings. You've no idea how I dreaded at first to cut up my gowns. It is the first time. . ." She was silent in momentary reverie. Then she turned upon me, her eyes snapping.

"You must take one. Surely you know some little girl who would adore one. You could give it to her for Christmas. Only six dollars I'm asking for them. It's such a ridiculous price. Just look at the materials of the dresses. And I had to buy the heads; I paid two dollars apiece just for those. Only six dollars, and you can choose whichever one you like, even to my adored little blonde."

I was suddenly shaken with vexation at myself. It was just my soft-headed sentimentality which got me into such scrapes, feeling sorry for people and letting myself be taken in by them. Confound this ugly old woman and her six-dollar dolls!

"I'm sorry," I said as bluntly as I knew how. "I've been working in the city only two months, and six dollars is a great deal of money to me. Besides, I don't know any little girls."

Immediately I was repentant. Her heavy old body seemed to crumple; the eyes welled with that hang-dog look of fear again. "Of course, dear child. Don't let me press you. You mustn't think I would urge you. But you do think they are beautiful, don't you? And a little girl would love one? Of course she would. You have no idea how much such materials cost when they were new. And the styling is perfect. Did I tell you how I used to go out in a carriage? I was a wonderful designer. You do think I could sell them, don't you dear?"

I had been brutal and I was ashamed of myself. Again I assured her that they were lovely beyond words, that of course she could sell them, that any little girl would adore them. Somebody might have to tell her that they wouldn't sell, but not I. I am not blessed with that difficult sort of courage.

"Thank you, dear. I am so glad of your opinion. Must

you go yet? But yes, of course, I have kept you so long. I hope you will come to see me again. I can't tell you how happy this little visit has made me. So few young people are sweet and thoughtful of the old. You will come again? Do promise to drop in in a day or two. I want to take your head size."

I wondered, as I ran up the stairs to the third floor and my belated supper, whether she was really in need of money. She had a much better room than I had.

Two weeks later, the landlord told me that Madam had fallen on the stairs and been taken to the hospital with a broken hip. He doubted that she would recover. So heavy and so old. I had never been back to pay my promised call. I was only twenty, and I was terribly afraid that she might make me a hat.

# #

THE RED SLAYER (3)

In the morning, the birds were chirping in the ragged apple tree alongside the house, and a low line of light streamed across the eastern horizon, the clump of pines on Purdy's place black and haloed against sunrise. David sat on the edge of his bed, and his skin tensed and crawled a little in the surprise and cool freshness of morning. He leaned forward to the open window, crossed the first and second fingers of both his hands in a cabalistic sign, and extended them toward the dawn. A sunburned boy, whose head wore a film of stiff fair hair, whose eyes were candid and solemn, he sat in the center of things and willed the sun to rise.

Slowly, in one low spot between a barn roof and the spearheads of the pines, the light intensified, and he drew upon it with all the strength of his need and the potency of his crossed fingers, a young fisherman of light, drawing up the sun, until a blazing thread appeared and crept upward and the blue-white streamers of light spread across the sleeping fields, above the mists on the bottom land, and touched the side wall of the house and the boy's hands and face.

David rose from the bed, spread his fingers wide, and made a deep salaam to the brightening east where the sun, clear of the earth line, palpitated with light, a broad silver coin quivering against the pallid sky. "I will always serve you, oh, light," he said in a breathy whisper and stood upright. "Oh, light," he repeated and stared at the beautiful fiery disk, burned toward it, returning life for life, and felt its whiteness stream into him and felt its faint warmth, while his eyes danced with glare and the white coins multiplied and clapped together and his eyes slowly filled with water. He squeezed his eyes tight, and little red and green coins danced against his lids, and he opened his eyes again, but the miracle was accomplished. The sun hung in full air in its accustomed remoteness, and he felt the power drain out of him. Again he bowed, without conviction this time; and he heard the back screen door slam and heard the clang of milk cans and the voices of his father and Mr. Willetts, the new hired man, and heard their footsteps on the gravel.

Walls closed around the young sun worshiper, and the spread of light was the commonplace of every day, the early hours of a school day. From the horizon of the day ahead, a black cloud of distaste began to form, and he remembered Mr. Pross. "The mean old sneak," he said to himself, but in his deeper mind, some more primitive resentment stirred. Mr. Pross was not to be pushed back into the uncomfortable but remote puzzle of the world of adults; he came prying and probing into the world of boyhood, stinging and exposing, laying all bare, "I hate you," David said aloud to the face of Mr. Pross, teacher of history, in the cool faint air of morning.

He found fresh underclothing laid out on the dresser top, and he put it on and pulled over it yesterday's blue jeans, bleached at the knees but ornamented with bright copper nailheads on the pocket corners.

His mother was moving from sink to table to glowing black stove with sharp but happy fury. She was a small woman, who accomplished amazing feats of cooking, sewing, gardening but who somehow managed to strew confusion behind her. Her wiry little body lashed out at the jumble of the kitchen, washing, pouring, stacking. She lifted the lid of the old-fashioned stove and thrust in a stick of oak wood, scolding at the fire: "Don't burn me, confound you. Keep your snapping little jaws down, There now!" She clattered the lid and shut the leaping flames in, vengefully. She saw David.

"What's been keeping you? Did you wash the sleep out of your eyes? Hurry along, get over there and eat. I can't keep breakfast on the fire all day. Did you put on that clean underwear I laid out?" As David passed her, she reached out a wiry brown arm and gave him a quick hug and kissed the back of his head. Her arm cradled him to her thin body and then pushed him on his way. "Go on, now eat."

Little Pris was sitting in her high chair, solemnly dipping spoonfuls of oatmeal from her pink bowl to the wooden tray, and Sammy was already scraping the edges of his cereal dish, the napkin that covered his front damp with milk droppings. The door opened, and the father came in, his mild eyes seeing none of them; gently smiling, he eased his way across the floor, stepping around Sammy's toys and avoiding the black cat, which was curled up near the stove. He ate absently, leafing through a book beside his plate. The mother's anger at the man's absence from all of them prickled through the room, and she clattered and thumped the pans furiously at the sink. Once, the man became aware of her rage and gravely followed her with his eyes, remembering how, in the night, she sank into sleep, muttering and gasping as though drowning and then abandoned herself as though sinking into bottomless waters. He returned to his book.

    David poured sugar over the oatmeal in his bowl, heaping the mountaintops high with granular snow and then flooding the bottom lands with a sea of milk, but the pleasure the miniature landscape gave him was thinned by the way his mother's actions cried out to have her anger recognized and by the patient resistance of his father, which was only a shade too mild to be insult.

    A knocking and thumping suddenly began under the kitchen floor, and the mother raised both hands to her loose brown hair and clutched it to emphasize her exasperation.

    "Something will have to be done," she cried. "Something will have to be done. Listen to that, Leonard--it's those woodchucks again. I don't see," she cried, "why this house has to be the center of attack by all the universe. I simply don't see it. It isn't as if you tried to do anything about it. I'm sure they're gnawing away at the foundations, and one of these days, the whole side of the house will collapse." And sure enough, as she spoke, from under the floor there was a slow grinding sound as of animal teeth gnawing upon wood.

    The man looked at the floor bemusedly. "Because there's no cellar under this side of the house, they're hard to get at," he said a bit shamefacedly. "They'll probably move out as soon as their family's raised. I saw her out on the grass with three or four young ones, yesterday. They're getting a pretty good size.

"We could be attacked by elephants for all you'd do about it," his wife said with prim irrelevancy. "It isn't enough that the bathtub's leaking and the telephone wire's broken. Have you mended that?"

"She has six babies, the woodchuck,' David corrected his father.

"They'll move out," the man said, running his fingers along his shaven sunburned jaw. "I have to go for the vet this morning, anyway. One of the cows looks to me to be a little bloated. I'll have to take the car." His voice faded away, retired from argument and from the pressure of his wife's insistence, and he let his eyes slide back again to the lucid prose of Emerson, and his face lighted.

This action moved the mother to a dangerous pitch. Her light-brown eyes grew dark, and she moved close to her husband, standing over him with arms akimbo, and reminded him that by taking a few minutes to patch the telephone wire, which was broken only a few feet from the house, just where it ran through the maple tree, he could save the price of the gasoline and could telephone the veterinarian instead of chasing, heaven only knew where, all over the country and getting no work done all morning. As she scolded, she swayed in the wind of her rage and her impotence, like a sailor on a tossed deck, her feet planted apart and her thin face strained with the terrors of shipwreck and the engulfing waters of poverty, her brightly striped apron girded to her waist, the fading flag of her courage and her despair. She demanded to know how much they already owed the veterinarian and when he thought they were ever going to manage to pay it.

Her husband came out of the book long enough to remind her, with a bruised gentleness, that what they owed wasn't as much as the price of a good cow.

Well, wasn't it possible to wait a few hours and see whether there was anything *really* the matter with the cow? But it was no use; she knew, she knew very well: He was just looking for an excuse to get in that car and go kiting up and down the country, like the eternal adolescent he was, and neglect everything and leave it all for her to do, and she could just cry--and here she wrung her hands and her face contorted with woe--when she realized that he could never understand what was important but always wanted to do such unnecessary things.

He was a city boy, her husband reminded her. He had to learn these things.

And how long, she wanted to know, was it going to take him to learn? He'd had five years, hadn't he? She wished he'd tell her what they were doing here on a farm, anyway. Just what on earth were they doing here? The man thought that they had come to the country for peace; at least, that was the original idea. And here his wife's eyes suddenly burned with tears, as if he had reproached her bitterly, and she ran from the room, only checking her flight to adjust the dampers on the stove to control the blazing fire.

David sat there, feeling miserable and hardly tasting his oatmeal, and little Pris began to whimper in her high chair. The father turned to her and from her fat neck untied the bib, wiped her mouth and hands with it, and set her gently on the floor. The baby laughed at him, and the man watched her with a wondering pleasure as if unable to assure himself entirely that she was real, and the baby plumped her firm little bottom solidly upon the floor and picked up her doll and began to play with its face.

The boy had to walk a mile to meet the school bus, and he plodded down the road, reluctant and a little injured from the clash at the breakfast table, and his shoulders began to feel the warmth of the climbing sun. After all, it hadn't been such a bad morning; he hadn't had to get up early to do the milking because now they had Mr. Willetts, who looked as dry and whiskery as a sheaf of barley and who would milk now, for a while, until he left, the way all their hired men did. David knew that Mr. Willetts wasn't much good and that his father would forget to pay him and would gradually forget to tell him what to do and that the man would grow idle and carping, until David himself would realize that it was no good and nothing was getting done and would have to take hold and start to do the chores again. Still, there would be a brief spell of freedom, and David, walking more briskly now, straightened his back, and his nostrils caught the damp sweetness of honeysuckle from the roadside, and he walked through sunlight where the shagbark hickories cast their elongated morning shadows upon the dust of the lane.

    David had wanted his father to drive him out to the bus, but his father had demurred, saying he wasn't ready to leave yet, he had to lay out the work for Mr. Willetts. The mother had come back quietly, drained of wrath, and had bustled about, making a stack of sandwiches and loading down David's lunch box, and there had been a moment of friendliness and bright, rattling busyness, full of pale sunlight and the smell of wood smoke from the slumbrous old stove, before the boy said a brusque good-by and opened the door onto the stillness of the waking world.

    Now he was glad he was afoot, with the dew still heavy on the wayside grasses, the weighted timothy, and the spraddled fescues, and with the wonderful smell of early morning, which would vanish upon the climbing of the sun. A breeze stirred a clump of sumac and wagged the brown satiny leaf clusters of the hickories, and the boy's heart galloped with a swift joy. He was filled with a sharpness of recollection, and hundreds of other mornings when he had walked as he walked now recurred and pressed upon him, mornings wet with spring greenery or with the sundried heat of August or with the crackling leaves and red gold going down to death of fall; and it came to him that not only in this life but in many lives he had walked in the dew of morning and known the touch of the earth, and he held his breath and saw a spider web on the sumac sparkle with blue and white fires.

Some lines came back to him which he had heard his father read yesterday morning at the table, when breakfast had been quiet and pleasant because Mr. Willetts had just arrived and things seemed to be picking up:

"If the red slayer think he slays,
Or if the slain think he is slain,
They know not well the...something (a word eluded him) . . . ways
I keep, and pass, and turn again."

David had thought the lines beautiful but confusing when he first heard them, but now, in the dew-washed morning, the words hinted to him, whispered strangely.

His father had explained that the poem meant that life was like a great wheel which turned without moving or changing its place, and David had remembered seeing, under fluorescent light, a spinning flywheel which appeared to his eyes to be standing still, with every line and bolt-head clear and unmoving, although his ears had caught the high whine of its turning and he could see the wide leather belt go flapping round and round. He had tried to see what the wheel had to do with life but he could not.

Now, briefly, he sensed the great wheeling cycle of the sun, and this hour of the awakening of day perpetually come new; the wet weeds, the little wind, the pale expanding sky. Through the long sweep of the past, this hour had been renewed, even the lumbering dawn man –Neanderthal -- with his shaggy forehead and peering eyes, had stopped and gazed upon this spread of light.

He walked again and watched the mists rise. A bittern broke precipitantly from the weeds ahead of him on the right, saw him, and waddled with clumsy speed along the crown of the road away from him. The ground alongside the road here was swampy, and the bittern suddenly skittered into a wide clump of rushes and disappeared. The great awkward bird had vanished so cleverly that, even though David had been watching her, he had to stand still for a minute or two, probing the reeds with his eyes before he spotted her, the stripes of her body not quite the same yellow as the bent swamp grasses, the neck thin and rigid, a rush among rushes. The bird did not stir, and he left her and went capering and jumping down the road, in a fine frenzy of joy and muscular passion and exuberance.

On the hard road at the end of the lane, Ronny Purdy was waiting, wearing a stiff pair of Levi's brittle with newness, and David set down his lunch box and leaped at him and pushed his chest, and the two boys wrestled valiantly on the grass. They stood up and their hands did some ineffectual brushing at their knees and the seats of their pants.

"I didn't have to milk," David said.

"I milked five cows," Ronny said pridefully. They stood silently beside their lunch boxes, watching three crows wheel and caw over the Purdy's field.

History class was at one o'clock, but Mr. Pross kept them waiting. The class sat sullen and unrelaxed, for old Prossy made a practice of lurking outside the door for the purpose of catching some venturesome roisterer emboldened by the absence of authority. Only Patsy Fleming, the daughter of the local millowner, was aware of immunity from the general threat and sat with one elbow crooked on the desk behind her and tossed her soft brown curls elegantly away from her neck, whispering secretly and with little slow smiles to Jane, in pigtails, her best friend, who leaned forward and giggled, sharing the happy aura of privilege.

In front of David sat fat Angie--Angelique Sotello --an unhappy newcomer to the community. She was one of the anomalous colony of foreigners who had been imported the year before to labor for the large orchardists of the upper end of the valley and who lived in a sort of gypsy camp of shanties and trailers in the patch of woods behind Schwartz's service station on the old turnpike. The girl spoke halting English and was older and larger than the other children, who did not like or accept her. Day after day, she sat cringing in her soft obesity, dull and foreign and ugly, her sorrowful black eyes the only beauty in her loose, fat face. The valley people, on the whole, resented the residence of these immigrants, and the strangers kept apart, their women never showing themselves outside the camp, the men congregating on Saturday nights in little groups on the square in town, natty, small-bodied, laughing, with sharp, threatening eyes.

Angie's shapeless back wore a bright-red sweater, not clean, with a rip in the worsted just below the neckline. An oval of dark skin showed through. Her tousled black hair was gray with nits near the scalp, and David moved back from contamination with her and looked again at Patsy in her green and blue Scotch plaid with the starched white collar, the lovely grace of the pretty elbow and the arrogant young head. He had loved her last year, and he wished she would look at him.

The door opened quietly, and Mr. Pross stood there, surveying the room. No one moved except Patsy, who languidly removed her elbow from her friend's desk and settled herself in her seat, tossing Mr. Pross a brief flattering smile. Mr. Pross moved to his desk, keeping his eyes on them, a little man with a womanish, unkind mouth and protruding eyes whose gaze was too bright and in whose depths a secret, cruel amusement lurked. He licked his lips and passed a hand over the top of his head, smoothing down the thin hairs which he kept plastered over his bald crown, and then he began to call the roll. He had a way of lingering on some of the names, as if sharing with the rest of the room a scarcely concealed ribaldry exposed in the absurdity of the Pennsylvania Dutch nomenclature: Stoops, Gobrecht, Klinedinst. And the worst of it was that he exerted some sort of fatal attraction upon them, which even hatred could not exorcise, and with his curious bright gaze upon them, they would smile guiltily and broadly, not looking up.

He taught them history in a harsh, finicking manner, without, David had discovered, knowing much of anything that wasn't in the book; and he insisted upon an exact regurgitation of the text, with a strong emphasis upon dates, where he was sure of their weakness.

In the man's heart must have rankled some soreness at the mediocrity of his endowments, the bitter joke that life had played upon him in building him small and unlovely and mean. His wife was a large woman, competent and dull, who arranged all his days in an unvarying regularity of meals, meetings, fifteen-minute calls on church members, newspaper reading, bedtime. His life held no joys. He lived in the same manner as the people about him, mediocre, censorious, cautious--but not contented. Some promise had not been fulfilled; he was the victim of some cheat on the part of life; and suffering from a festering sense of disappointment, he found in the helplessness of the children under him the means of venting his sour spleen upon the world, of passing on the sting. He was careful of the words he used--words might be quoted. The venom lay in intonation, in a twist of the lip, in the low snicker, the implication of mockery. The chalk dust of the smeared blackboards, the pink, green, blue, and orange patchwork of countries and seas on the thumb-marked maps which pulled down from their rollers with whining reluctance, the smells of ink and long-worn clothing and the jelly sandwiches of noon — all these resented commonplaces framed the arena in which Mr. Pross, here only armed with power and advantage, pressed on to injure in unequal warfare.

He had his particular butts among the children, of whom David was one. David had made the mistake, early in the school year, of volunteering some information and had thus done violence to Mr. Pross's authority. The class had been studying primitive man, and David had offered some scraps of knowledge which he had gleaned from an examination of *The Golden Bough* in his father's library: Some anthropologists thought the first human society was a matriarchy. The women had the power, and the kings were merely husbands of an earth goddess who was supposed to be the mother of everything, and the kings were killed every year at planting time and at harvest time. It was a kind of magic, primitive people thought, killing a man so the crops would grow. The ones who did it were the first priests.

    David had first become aware of a glad astonishment in the teacher's eyes; and then, in a quick reversal of attitude, the man had broken into his tittering little laugh and had begun to question David, in a probing fashion, about his parents. Was he correctly informed that David's father held the degree of Master of Arts? David, bold in his innocence, had said that his mother had one too. Mr. Pross had turned to the class, and something very bad had taken place. It began with almost fawning congratulations upon the boy's background and then sly innuendoes of unusual sorts of knowledge that must exist and be discussed in such a home. David appeared to be prepared to inform them all, said the soft scathing voice, about many matters of which they would have remained in ignorance without his aid, things that had been left out of the book -- perhaps designedly left out of the book, since there were some facts of history which Mr. Pross had a feeling the parents of some of these young people, particularly the parents of some of the young ladies (with a snigger), would not care to have their children exposed to. David had sat there, besmirched and blushing hotly, but outraged too, because a relationship had been violated, something offered in honesty had been twisted and made foul.

    His teacher's words, as he had tried to repeat them that night to his mother, had sounded harmless and even just, and he could in no way convey to her the humiliation he had been put to. . "But why should you be ashamed of having educated parents, David? And what did you tell the class? From *The Golden Bough*? I'm afraid that's hardly the sort of material for junior high school. You'd better try reading something else for a change." She had closed a door in his face and shut herself in with the adults, in that privileged world where Mr. Pross could range unchecked in slyness and vindictiveness and cruel power.

The man's face had, for months now, troubled the boy's sleep. It was Mr. Pross's smile that appeared on the faces of the tarantulas and black wasps of David's insect dreams in which the giant bodies of spiders, mosquitoes, and bees burst through the frail window screens of his house, their stingers quivering for his meat, and frozen, he fled on a sled drawn by no visible hand through the rooms of the house, with body paralyzed and bound, unable to move an arm before the onslaught of beaks and prongs that swarmed upon him, the mottled, drooping abdomens bloated with the dark poisons of the night.

Now he sat at his desk, his feet heavy in his shoes, and kept his eyes withdrawn from Mr. Pross, until gradually his gaze became absorbed in the dark mat of Angie's hair, a greasy tangled net in which insects lurked, a net that could be a web built by some hairy-legged thing...

"David McLaughlin." Mr. Pross's voice reached him on its way down the roll call, and David, lurking out of sight on the path of Angie's uneven part, muttered in response, "Spiders."

There was silence, a silence that waited after the first shock and that now squirmed and giggled with impending catastrophe. Mr. Pross was caught in shock as sharply as were the students. His mouth sagged open for a long moment and he seemed to test the air as if uncertain of the sound his ears had brought to him. Then he began to walk, with infinite slowness, down the aisle toward David's desk his eyes fixed and preternaturally bright. Without quite knowing that he was doing so, David rose to his feet to meet him.

The man made no sound; the abnormally bright eyes clung to David's and drew closer in a probing fixity that sheered away the boy's safety, broke down the winded hills and sunny valleys, the fire and folk comforts of his life, and left him open to the wolf stalk of madness -- eyes cold with an

Eleven Stories ... plus

iciness far beyond rage, which touched the coiling unrealities of nightmare, which sent the boy's spirit running wildly where all the decencies and kindliness of everyday life must be abandoned, lost, sacrificed to the encroaching threat. He forsook all his bulwarks.

"It's her hair," he said and pointed at Angie. "It's full of spiders."

The betrayal saved him. Mr. Pross was thrown off balance, he lost the advantage of attack, he was no longer formidable. The class snickered and gazed gleefully at one another. And Mr. Pross, still set to punish, knowing himself outmaneuvered, turned on the sacrificial victim offered him. He turned in frustration and spite, for the sake of David, who had temporarily slipped out of his reach; and as he spoke and fat Angie cowered, he realized the helplessness of his prey and was the more scathing because he had not recognized her vulnerability before this. So David could not keep his eyes off Angelique? Mr. Pross could see why, but he would not go so far as to suggest that even David found her attractive. The teachers should have done something about her before this. The girl was foul, she was stupid, she was outlandish, an alien demanding time and attention that should better have been given to American boys and girls. She came here in her filth; even an animal, a she-dog, would be cleaner...

This time, Mr. Pross had gone too far. With a moaning wail, Angie lumbered out of the confines of her desk and fled the classroom, weeping. She edged out the door blindly, sidewise; her shapeless rump caught momentarily against the doorjamb, escaped. How was Mr. Pross to know that the girl had no mother, that her father had brought her alone, of his children, to the new land, to protect her in her softness and witlessness? How was Mr. Pross to comprehend anything of her need? He did not know how to love anyone.

Nor did Angie's flight actually discomfit him. He adjusted the lapels of his herringbone coat and, by shooting a last jibe at David, managed to shift the blame for the splenetive outbreak: "Why don't you follow her and tell her you're sorry for what you said about her?"

David was almost impelled by his own grief and wrath and by a heavy sense of shame to follow the girl. But it was too much. Mr. Pross had no right to abuse poor old Angie, but it was David himself who had offered her as a scapegoat, tossed her to the stinging wasp of the night. He should let her know he was sorry. He hadn't meant it; but he couldn't. To expose himself to the ridicule of his classmates by going after her, he could have managed--if it had been anyone but Angie. But the big girl's unkempt person strongly offended him; her smell, her dirt, her soft fatness filled him with distaste; and he was ashamed of his own fastidiousness. He sat squirming in pain, indignation, and self-hatred until the bell released him. As the class filed from the room, Patsy's eyes touched him with a glint of knowing and David, shocked, discovered a wickedness in her which acknowledged him as a companion. In that instant, he disliked her intensely.

At home, there was no respite to be sought from his mother. She was ironing clothes, a task which always put her in a temper, and she was hot and tired. She began to complain the moment David put his books down on the kitchen sideboard. His father was still out somewhere in the car, hadn't been home for lunch, hadn't been home all day, and how she was expected to manage all alone like this and with everything piling up, she wished somebody would tell her.

David hated the way she always criticized his father, but he disliked seeing her so unhappy, and he knew how things had piled up. He went up to his room and found it trim and neat, the painted floor washed, the bed smooth, his things carefully stacked on their shelves; the care with which she tended him made him even more miserable.

He took from its corner the new .22 rifle which he had been given for his birthday. Since he was now twelve, he would be allowed to go hunting with his father when the season opened next fall, and in the two months he had owned the rifle, he had practiced diligently, using a tin-can target set against the cement side of the old hog house. Now he loaded the gun from a box of shots in his desk and, first laying the rifle carefully on the shingles, climbed out the north window of his room onto the low shed roof of the kitchen and carried the gun to the far edge of the roof, below which the woodchucks had their hole.

He had been observing the animals for weeks. First, there had been only the big bloated mother, and then she had disappeared briefly and appeared again, looking flabby, and shortly her young, fat with fur, had followed her on little forays from the hole. It interested David that the woodchucks ate none of the meadow grass around the doorway to their underground retreat. Weeds and timothy grew high there, but narrow runnels through the rough growth led out to the feeding grounds where the old chuck browsed upon greenstuffs. The mother always emerged from the hole first, darting her snout into the air as if to sniff the wind for danger; and only after she had climbed out and squatted like a loaf of coarse fur on the grass, did the babies creep out to join her. Sometimes David had waited an hour, sitting on the kitchen roof or peering from the window, before she would venture forth. She never came out when he was in the meadow.

The boy had no affection for the family of shy rodents; he did not think of them as personalities as he did of the farm animals. But something in them made him glad; he welcomed their self-containment, their inviolability, the life that fulfilled itself in them, in the same way in which he rejoiced in the blue dawn light, in the strength and structure of plants. He always turned silent and contemplative and lost himself in observation of them.

Today his purpose had changed and the relationship had become damaged, as all relationships had suffered and changed during the past unpleasant hours. The moss on the edges of the shingles was dry and spiny where his hand rested on it, and he thought of Angie and his ugly words about her hair, and he wanted to feel repentant but was able to feel little except revulsion. Still, Angie was only dirty; it was he himself who was bad. He had been a filthy liar and had done her shameful hurt. He was bad, and Patsy, who did not mind what had happened, who even relished it and had meant to reward him for it, was bad. But Mr. Pross was the worst, Mr. Pross, who liked to hurt people, who waited for chances, who had drawn David into inner honesty which, uninvited, acted as castigator in David's mind as he struggled to reshape and explain away the horrid hour, spoke quietly and said that he could have endured the assault of Mr. Pross and lived through it. Mr. Pross had never hit anyone. But a panic in his bones told him that such endurance was beyond his power. It was not of being hit that he was afraid. He was a boy and Mr. Pross was a man. He saw, in his mind, the cold glaring eyes bearing down upon him, and he grew sick with weakness. He would never be able to enter that classroom again -- if the man looked at him, he would vomit from disgust and rage and helplessness. He was lost in his cowardice and in his hatred, and the future hemmed him in. The sunlight before his eyes was a red blur, and the grass, a matted tangle without shape.

    A moment arrived when the snout of the woodchuck poked tentatively from the burrow and withdrew. He remembered his mother's despair and thought vaguely of what he was here for, on the roof with the .22. Those woodchucks -- old groundhogs was all they were, really – were becoming a holy mess of a nuisance with all that chawing under the floor, and now there'd be more and more of them, with the young ones getting half as big as the mother. The heavy female put out her head, and her short forepaws clung to the edge of the hole. David watched her in sore and resentful silence, not really paying her much attention. She gave two humping lurches and was out on the grass, her head turning, her nose seeking the wind. She moved forward, stopped, shifted her body, settled herself, and turned her face toward the burrow. And David lifted his gun. Her eyes were very bright, expressionless, staring. If David had old Pross's snouty face in front of a gun sight like that, it would be all he wanted. He would show no mercy. He would look at those beady eyes and hate him, hate him to the very point of death, and he'd squeeze the trigger, squeeze the trigger.

The gun went off with a crack that was not very loud, and David felt an instant of furious release and vindication. The woodchuck drooped and jerked all over several times and then slowly slid on the shallow incline and rolled onto its back and lay there, fat and slack, the little forepaws curled and wilted against its belly. David laid down the gun and moved to the lower edge of the roof, swung himself down along the drainspout, and dropped lightly to the ground. He walked over and touched the chuck with his foot, and the head rolled. He had got her right through the eye--pretty fancy shooting. He picked her up by a hind foot and caught her under the back with his left hand. She was warm and heavy and very limp. He would take her down and throw her in to the hogs.

But suddenly he could not do it. She was so limp. Where had the life gone that had made her sniff and scurry and jerk her head only a minute ago? He had never killed anything before, and although he had seen dead animals, this time it was not the same. He wanted to take her out into the deep grass and bury her, somehow, back where she belonged. There was very little blood; yet the inertness and weight of her in his hands told him that he had gone too far in interfering with her. It didn't matter what his mother thought about it, he was not going to kill the rest of them. He put the warm body down in a depression in the field and pulled several handfuls of tall grasses and laid them over her like a blanket. He went back to the roof and put his gun away without cleaning it.

He did not want to tell his mother what he had done, and he walked out to the maple tree at the corner of the house and inspected the broken telephone wire. One end of the wire, still dangled across a branch where the line had passed through the foliage of the tree; the other lay curled in uneven spirals on the lawn. David found a ball of twine and pair of pliers in the woodshed and carried them out to the lawn. He bent the end of the coiling wire and fastened a slipknot of twine upon it. Then, tucking the ball of twine into his belt, he climbed the tree and slowly drew the paid-out cord up to him, and the wire followed. The whole thing turned out to be almost too simple; there was more slack in the wire than he had expected, and he wouldn't even have to splice in a new piece. He brought the two ends of the wire together, bent one over the other, wound each back upon itself. With a pinch from the pliers, he made the joining tight. The wire stretched smoothly, with very little sag in it, and hung clear of the branches.

He wished there were something else to do, but he didn't want to go down to the barn and help Mr. Willetts because that would get him started expecting David to do half the chores all the time, and chores would start soon enough anyway. He climbed higher in the tree to one of his favorite perches, where the wind moved the branches, and settled himself in the crook of a limb. He tried to play one of his childhood games and pretend that the tree was the rigging of a tall ship and that he was his great-great-grandfather who had gone around the Horn and sailed to China, but the tree remained a tree and the bark was rough and the leaves were green and small and pale in the afternoon sunlight. A puff of dust whirled upon the county road and moved toward the farmhouse and became a car, his father coming home. But David did not climb down or call to him.

A sweet, yet bitter sadness weighed upon his spirit, and he kept thinking of how the woodchuck had felt in his hands. He twisted around on his seat so that he could look over to the burrow, and he saw that the young woodchucks were out. Five of them were there--no, all six--and they were milling around in confused little circles.

They are hunting for her, he thought; *they are hunting for their mother, and she is lying out there, dead, and she will never come back to them. I'm the one who did it to them. I'm the one who did it to her. I killed an innocent woodchuck in cold blood.* His throat hurt, and he leaned his face against the bark and cried with slow, aching sobs.

After a while, he slid down the trunk and wandered

Eleven Stories ... plus

restlessly out through the pasture to the pasture spring under the big black walnut, which was the last tree to leaf out in the spring, the first to drop its foliage and stand bare in the fall. He lay flat and drank from the spring, placing his mouth against the surface of the slow-purling water; then he washed his hot face. Some change had come over him which troubled him with a sense of loss deeper than guilt. He did not go up to the house until the dinner bell had rung twice.

As soon as he entered the kitchen, he knew something had happened; the house was filled with excitement and shock and with little waves of the embarrassed enjoyment which accompanies a horror that does not touch us closely. Even his father was excited in a pained way. It was his mother who told him, making her voice low and mournful as was proper, but relishing the telling, nevertheless. Something dreadful had happened. The telephone had rung a little while ago (she did not even stop to wonder how the telephone line had been repaired), and it was Mr. Purdy to tell Mr. McLaughlin that one of the teachers at the high school had been killed. One of David's teachers, Mr. Pross. He had been stabbed in the heart with a knife by one of those men from the laborers' camp--the man had waited outside his house when he came home at five o'clock--and the killer was in jail and would be tried for murder. David's father rubbed his fingers along his jaw line and asked David gravely whether anything had happened at school. It appeared that the murderer insisted to the police that there had been a wicked insult to his daughter. He said Mr. Pross had called his daughter a she-dog and, back home in his own country, such a word spoken to a girl was an invitation to death. Did David remember? Had anything like that occurred?

David listened through long, sweeping waves of panic. Mr. Pross was dead, lying warm and limp, his head rolling loose on his dead neck. Upon this picture, there played a faint surface glimmer of relief; some word whispered that David had escaped now, Mr. Pross had been taken care of by some force apart from himself. But deep in him stirred his own terrible dark embroilment in the crime. He had done it, he had caused it, his own hatred and cowardice had linked in power and brought it to pass. His father had to ask him twice what Mr. Pross had said to Angelique. Had he called her a she-dog? David came up out of darkness and said yes, he thought so, he remembered it. Somehow he wanted to explain that Mr. Pross had not meant to injure her so deeply, but that would have been a lie. Mr. Pross wanted to hurt all of them. But even Mr. Pross had been frightened for a minute by what he had said. It was impossible to explain this to his parents. He wondered whether he should mention his own part in the trouble, but that dark whirlpool of guilt sucked at his heart with terror and would not come up to the light. If he told them, if he said, "I did it first. I said she had spiders in her hair," what would they think? What would they say? They might look grave and disapproving, but they would explain it away, dismiss him with a gentle reproof. Or would they? Would they believe that the guilt was his? *I was the one who pointed out Angie; I showed her dirt and her softness to him. It is my fault that Angie moaned and ran and that her father burned with fire and that Mr. Pross is lying limp and heavy and warm and dead. I am the one who should be sitting in the murderer's cell, waiting to die.*

    David's father nodded his head solemnly and said Ronald Purdy had also confirmed the father's story. But it was doubtful that it would do poor Sotello much good. It was a mistake, a grave mistake, this importing men of different folkways into a society that enjoyed a milder ethic and then punishing them for not understanding this country's twentieth-century mores. The poor fellow had acted in accordance with right as he had learned it, but that wasn't going to exonerate him in this community. The community was tightly integrated, sullenly provincial. Pross had been respectable, a churchgoer, a local man. Murder itself was too far outside the pattern. "We know not what we do," he muttered, and his face was gentle.

    David's mind kept circling around his own act--his own two acts, which somehow were intermingled. *If any of the boys, or Patsy, tells what I did, I will admit it; but that won't make any difference in the punishment. And if no one tells, I am safe, and Patsy will glint her eyes at me, and only she and I will know this guilt which I will carry with me all the days of my life. But only I will know all of it, only I will know the real murder I did. What if I told them that I aimed a gun and willed Mr. Pross to die and it went off and he died, just the way I wanted, and the woodchuck died too; I sacrificed her so that Mr. Pross would die, but I meant to hit him?*

He was unable to eat, and his parents were quiet, wondering, and cautious with him. When his mother rose to take the younger children up to bed, he got up too. While she was washing their hands and faces, he toiled upstairs to his room, stood at the window awhile, and then opened it and went out to sit on the roof.

The sun was going down in a red line of light against a clear green sky, which promised a fair day tomorrow. The little woodchucks were out wandering on the grass. David's whole mind felt empty, and the hush and clear birdcall of evening were remote from him. Nothing would approach his heart. The woodchuck in her fur and softness lay out there under her blanket of grass, and he knew with finality that it was she he had murdered, it was not Mr. Pross. It was Mr. Pross he had aimed at, Mr. Pross for whom the deadly bullet was intended, but it was this heavy, gentle furred life he had struck down.

Something that had power in the world had decided -- a wheel had turned strongly and removed Mr. Pross without his help, without needing his help. What he had done was in some deep way more wrong than the act of the enraged father of Angelique, more evil than his own betrayal of the girl. For it was true that for an instant he had seen the night spiders in her hair. His evil-doing was a murder without motive, an unclean sacrifice. He had not remained true to the world that unfolded about him in the hours when, pure in heart, he had wandered in loneliness. He had mixed two worlds; he had not kept safe the world of dawn and the turning seasons and the innocent animals. He had chosen to intrude with murderous weapon, aimed by his own sick hatred, upon this secret world that wheeled by its own sure law, serene and remote from love and hate, from hope and fear. He had mingled it with the marred and muddied doings of people. All his life, even in maturity, he was to yearn, in moments of quiet, for that hush of the opening day, the breath of pure being, the sense of the great wheel turning. But humanity had touched him now; he was caught up on the world of guilt.

    He sat huddled together, his chin on his knees, full of sullen pain and despondency, and watched the sun go down without his help. The red ball dwindled and faded below the dark hill line, and the sunset shot its red flares into the ice-green sky. He sat there until the light was gone and his back was cold, and his aching eyes watched a great door swing shut, with the last light, irrevocably upon the lost world of nature and of blessing.

# # #

Passing Bell (4)

Harriet did not know how she had got into Cousin Margaret's basement, and it was so impossibly cluttered, not like Margaret at all, such endless heaps of florists' boxes tumbled every which way, and she thought, "Why, how silly of Margaret. It could start a fire." And just then the fire started, a little flash of sparks on the electric wiring that ran along the white-washed beams above her head. The fire crept along the wire in a trickle of low flame, but it didn't seem to be catching anything else until it reached a drooping net of pale cobwebs and flared up into that, but she put up her hand and was able to wipe the cobwebs down without burning herself. Only, now the fire was spreading: there were ever so many feet of wire burning, and she thought painstakingly, "I'll have to call the fire department." It was then she saw the newspaper, a big thick fold of newspaper wedged above the wires at one end of the beam where the fire was just reaching. Her heart jumped in panic and fury and she knew at once: Leila had done it, Leila had put it there, Leila wanted the house to burn down.

She reached up and took hold of the newspaper and pulled, and it came down burning, and she looked around her and put it in a watering-pot and put it out. Oh, wicked Leila! But the flames were still burning along the wires and she lifted her head and began to breathe on them with her mouth open--*carbon dioxide puts out fires*--only her breath didn't affect the flames at all. She thought of the watering-pot, but she could see that the insulation along the wires was very old and worn, and she remembered in time that you can't put water on an electric fire, so she knew she would have to go up and get the fire department after all, and she looked around, and there weren't any stairs.

Her heart was still beating fearfully, but she was in the garden, and there were endless crowds of people as if there were a garden party; only it wasn't festive, and whenever she came near any of the groups of people they slowly turned their backs on her. She knew, somehow, that there was something immensely important that she must tell someone, but she couldn't remember what it was; and then Cousin Margaret came by, hurrying, and whispered to her as she went past: "Don't look like that, my pet; they'll notice. You can't afford to wear your heart on your sleeve." Margaret had on a wide stiff hat with daisies on it, and she smiled from under the brim with her wise, shrewd eyes as she sailed away.

    Harriet began walking a little, this way and that, not being sure where she wanted to go, and then she came to the big cluster of blooming yucca by the side of the arbor and she stood there because this was the right place, and there was a little wind in the creamy yucca bells. A small boy in a bright blue suit was crouched on the grass, cutting a mouse into slices with a shiny pocketknife, and the mouse whimpered. She looked around, but nobody was paying any attention to him, and she said out loud, "Don't do that." The boy looked up at her with dark calculating eyes, and then he bent down and went on cutting into the mouse.

    She was terribly frightened and began to whimper. One of the groups of people broke apart then, and a man in a white summer jacket turned with a slow swing of the shoulder that she joyfully recognized, and a sweet peace flooded her. It was Harry, and he saw her and walked quickly toward her and came up to her, and put his hands harshly and tenderly on her shoulders and said softly, "How's my girl?" She said, "Oh, Harry, I've been so frightened," and she pressed her face against the breast of his coat, and his arms went round her and held her fiercely against him. She said into his coat, "I thought I wouldn't meet you," and he put one hand against her hair and said in slow tones like a bell tolling: "There is only one meeting, my dearest, ever, for any of us."

    But when she looked up, at that, his eyes were not sorrowful, but were bright with joy, and he reached out and pulled a flower globe from the yucca. A sweet pain choked her throat, for she knew exactly what was going to happen next. He began to smile and his eyes were teasing, and he said, "You know, you have always reminded me of a flower, with that cluster of curls, but I've never known which one. Margaret says a hyacinth, but that's too stubby for your slenderness, and the petals are too tight for your hair. This is it," he said, moving the yucca stem so that the bells shivered, "clear and clean, and a lovely tumble of curls."

    They looked at each other and laughed, and their laughter was like the sound of white bells breaking. ". . . and responsive," he whispered, looking down at her, his eyes suddenly stricken, urgent and suffering. "See how she trembles when I touch her?" He fixed the yucca flower in her hair. "That's to keep you rooted here until I get back," he said. "You'll excuse me for a minute?" He moved away
and then stopped and looked around at her. "Don't go away," he said.

    "No, I won't," she called. "I won't go away." She was so happy but it wouldn't do to watch him out of sight because that was unlucky.

    When she opened her eyes the crowds were pressing down upon her all at once, and they swarmed around her until, try as she might, she couldn't stand still, and they began pushing her toward the house and she couldn't see the yucca plant.

    When she stumbled into the living room of the house, the room was dusky and there were only great square blocks instead of furniture and there were no windows in the walls. Leila was sitting on one of the blocks, sewing on a sewing machine, and she looked up and said firmly "Sit down, Harriet." Harriet sat down, and Leila went on sewing furiously, with the machine sawing and clattering, but she never once took her secret and clouded eyes from Harriet's face.

    I mustn't let her guess I'm waiting for Harry, thought Harriet. But Leila knew. Leila was sewing on a bright blue suit for little Harry, and she held it up for Harriet to see. But what Harriet saw was that there was something Leila was hiding, some terrible and deadly knowledge that Harriet had forgotten, that she must remember, while the clouded, secret eyes wouldn't let her remember.

"You must look at my new buttonhole machine," Leila said. "You never saw anything like it. Harry buys me all the machines I want," she said, and she began to make one buttonhole after another, very fast.

Harriet kept her eyes glued to the racing circle of buttonholes, but beneath her ribs a cold apprehension began to spread and spread, and suddenly her rapid heart stopped beating within her breast and was stricken by an ice-cold and unendurable stab of pain, and she almost knew, and fought against knowing.

Just at that moment the flames shot up all around the walls, and Leila's eyes let go their secrets and were greedy and satisfied and naked. And Harriet saw that she had failed to remember the fire, but it didn't matter. It was too late now. She and Leila looked at each other, and they both knew. Their eyes held and held. There wasn't any antagonism any longer between their eyes, meeting; and no regret, and no forgiveness; only honesty and in each her bitter, deadly knowledge.

Leila's eyes shifted slyly towards the burning walls, and Harriet suddenly grasped her danger. Leila had meant to hold her here past all chance of escape. The flames howled and hemmed them in. The furniture blocks began to burn up furiously, one at a time. The wood was charring around her feet. *Oh, the flames! Oh, the fierce, burning world. Harry, save me!* With a ghastly roar, the floor buckled and dropped her into fire.

Harriet shook open her eyes upon the half light of a clammy dawn. A wild rain was battering the windows of her bedroom behind the starched curtains. A crack of thunder sounded, very near. It must have been thunder that had wakened her. And she had slept, after all. The full box of sleeping pills lay on the bedside table, and she had not taken them.

She slipped out of bed and walked to the window.

Down by the arbor the yucca drooped, heavy with raindrops. And Harry was dead ... dead ... dead. She had not known what flowers to send for the funeral and had left it up to Margaret. And Margaret had sent tuberoses ... tuberoses ... *The dear desire in his eyes, in her dream, and the familiar way he turned his head. Oh, Harry, don't leave me.* Her bare feet were very cold upon the floor. She thought, shaking in her nightgown, that she must break a single stalk of yucca and carry it by herself and lay it upon Harry's grave, and then she looked at the familiar wet roofs of the small town and the windows behind which waited all the watching eyes, and knew that she would not.

#　　#　　#

MR. PAN (5)

> He ordered black dragons with gold tongues
> to be embroidered on a coat of vermilion

Mr. Pan was a man who died every day. Mr. Pan lived near the wall of the city in a small house with a red lacquered gate and a door set with tiles tinted blue like shallow water, on which were enameled patterns of flowering rice and of water reeds. In the garden were a clump of pale green bamboos and a dark green banana tree. A pretty goldfish pool lay in the shade of the bamboos, a pool with a rim of light green tile decorated in patterns of plum blossom and displaying the six characters of an ancient poem:

> When no foot approaches,
> The plum blossom is without fragrance.

Within the house were clean straw mats, two carved chairs, and six delicate blue-and-white teacups.

Yet every day Mr. Pan died in a most anguishing manner. When he arose in the morning and knelt before the basin to wash his face in clear water, he pondered that, being weak without his breakfast, he was almost certainly about to faint, and he saw how his body would slide forward and his face drop in the wide basin and he would be dead of suffocation before a neighbour should come in to discover him. Indeed, it might be a day or two before he was discovered, and in the meantime his body would turn blue and the ants would crawl over it, so that the neighbour, entering in a friendly and carefree manner, would discover a most horrid sight. Upon this reflection, Mr. Pan would rise from his knees and open the window before he washed, so that a passerby might notice the trouble within.

When Mr. Pan dressed and a loose thread from the seam of his trousers tickled his skin, he would seize with two fingers a bit of the cloth of the garment and, quivering, pull it away from his flesh while he waited for the sting of the poisonous spider or scorpion which had crawled into the snug folds of the cotton during the night.

Sometimes when he had been working with his hands, Mr. Pan would discover upon his palm a bit of loose skin from a blister or callus, and he would try it tremulously with a fingernail and find it without sensation. Then the hand of fear would squeeze his heart, for lack of sensation is the telltale sign of leprosy, and he would imagine that he was infected and that he must leave his pretty house and wander among hedgerows, shunned by men. He would feel the bite of the frost and see the remote and compassionless glitter of the night stars out of a black sky, and would twist his rags about him against the wind.

When he walked in the street and saw a flagpole with a pennon or a lantern blowing gently at its tip, he would become the climber who had set the bit of paper there, and he would feel his hands slip on the smooth pole and his knees fail to grip and he would plummet awfully through space, his hands clutching at the yielding air, and hear the crunch of his bones on the packed earth.

When the kettle boiled for his tea, he would tremble lest the brazier tip upon the mat and the walls flame up and he run screaming from his house with his hair afire. When the house creaked in the night, he lost his courage, dreaming that a thief drew near among the shadows, with bared knife.

Even when he stood in clear sunlight in his peaceful garden and looked out beyond the city walls at the hills that were blue as rare porcelain, with here and there the square of a field or the red dot of a house, he would remember that in times past this had been volcanic country, and he would feel the molten river creeping beneath the earth at his feet and feel the molten consuming roar of the eruption.

One morning it happened that Mr. Pan upon awakening coughed three times. Now he realized at last that he had caught a deadly disease, and when he had washed, and brewed his tea, he crawled back into his bed, for the terrible lassitude in his body told him that he must now count as loss each rising of the sun over the earth's rim. During the restless day he coughed three more times; whereupon he dragged himself feebly from his pallet and made a poultice of banana leaves for his chest. In the still, late afternoon, when the breeze no longer stirred the leaves of the bamboo in the garden, footsteps sounded on the stones outside, and a messenger appeared in the doorway to tell Mr. Pan that his only sister, who lived in another city a day's journey distant, believed herself to be dying and wished to see her brother before her eyes closed for the last time.

"Alas," said Mr. Pan, "I too am dying. I am far wasted with the blood-spitting disease and will not many times see the sun rise to warm the earth. Tell my sister that we shall enter the Great Void together."

Five days later on a morning golden with sun, when Mr. Pan had recovered from the disease, the messenger appeared again and informed him that his sister was dead. Now Mr. Pan was filled with shock and his knees actually grew weak, for he had not really envisioned his sister dying. His eyes filled with tears, and he went to the clothes chest and took out a white mourning garment and put it on and fastened at his waist a purse full of money for travelling. Thus he accompanied the messenger to his sister's house.

When the funeral rites were accomplished and the last shred of devilpaper had blown away on the wind, Mr. Pan came back with the family to his sister's house, and there for the first time he took note of his sister's three small children, sitting sad-eyed by the door in their wadded coats. There were two little girls and a very small boy. The children's faces were smudged and their black eyes trembled with tears, but they were bravely attempting not to cry.

"Let your tears fall," Mr. Pan told them. "The tears of sorrow water the flower of memory." As the words came from his mouth, Mr. Pan found somewhere tucked away in his mind, the remembered face of his sister, lovely as a plum blossom.

Mr. Pan's brother-in-law had died two years before. His sister had not married into a fortunate house, and the two old parents had no more than enough silver to fill their stomachs with rice and to warm the dark little house, which opened only upon the public street.

"Let the children come to live with me," said Mr. Pan. "When the young plant sprouts it must be watered and set in the sun." And he remembered the golden light of the sun that filled his garden.

The little girls were named White Almond Flower and Little Willow Tree; the name of the boy was Virtue of Tranquility. During the journey their eyes were shy and their lips did not open. For a week they were shy, and then it seemed to them that the morning light which turned the window frame rosy had always shone on them through this same window, and they were at home and became noisy.

Virtue of Tranquility brought to his uncle a splintered shoot of the bamboo which he had broken off, and White Almond Flower came crying, for she had fallen and cut her knee on the shattered stalk.

Mr. Pan washed the knee, which was round and sweet as a yellow peach, and put on it a clean strip of white cloth as a bandage. "This time you must not cry," he told her. "The body of a woman will keep the scars of many pains her mind has forgotten."

At the same time he saw on his own arm two small scars whose source he could not recall. "The bamboo climbs swiftly up the lines of the sunlight," he told his nephew. "Let us permit it to grow as it wishes."

The two little girls emptied a bowl of tea into the goldfish pool, and the goldfish died. The boy took a stone from the path and scratched a crosshatched pattern on the red lacquer of the gate. "Poor little ones," thought Mr. Pan, "they have never seen beautiful shapes and do not know how to regard them," and he made them a boat of green-and-silver paper to float on the rainwater tub.

When a nobleman's carriage passed, he took the children into the street to watch the horses. The manes were plaited and tied with golden threads from which tiny bells of gold and silver hung and tinkled. The horses bowed their wide necks in moving arches, and their gilded hoofs lifted high and trod down firmly.

In her tenth summer, Little Willow Tree was bitten on the foot by a serpent. Mr. Pan cut the flesh with the steel edge of a knife and sucked the wound, pressing his lips against the ivory instep. He bathed the wound in cold tea and made a poultice, and as he held the poultice securely to the slender arched foot, Little Willow Tree looked at him trustfully. Mr. Pan felt frightened that he had not done enough, and he examined the firm flesh of the leg to see whether it was swelling or turning colour; but immediately he noticed that the poultice had grown warm, and he hurried to make a fresh one.

In that same summer, in the month when the herons come to the river banks, Mr. Pan decided that the children were to be taught to read and write; not the boy only, but the girls as well. Accordingly he paid two pieces of silver from the chest to an indigent scholar, who taught the children for an hour every morning when the grass in the garden was bright with dew and the shadows of the bamboo were long.

When the children quarreled over their games in the evening, Mr. Pan steeped a steaming bowl and persuaded the three to join him in a circle to drink tea from the blue-and-white cups and recite poems. They recited many old poems and some newer ones:

> The present is the palm of your hand.
> The future is a mirror
> Standing at the back of your mind.

> Listen to the voice of the pine needles
> When the wind is still.

> Do not have hope, do not have fear,
> For neither one is able to hear the frogs calling
> From the green pool among the rushes
> As dusk clouds the water.

Sometimes the boy recited the poem from the rim of the goldfish pool.

White Almond Blossom had a face shaped to a perfect oval, and when she was fifteen years old she was as lovely as the sickle moon in a mist. Mr. Pan found for her a husband from an honourable family and gave for her dowry sixteen pieces of silver and a bolt of yellow silk.

Little Willow Tree had a snub face like a little round pan and smiling eyes which made the observer smile in return. Her uncle arranged her engagement to a likeable young man, the eldest son of an official; and when the season of autumn fires had come and the wedding was celebrated, her dowry was eighteen pieces of silver and a silk coverlet of cutwork pattern embroidered with butterflies and willow branches.

Now it was the boy's turn. Mr. Pan questioned his nephew and learnt that Virtue of Tranquility, the youth of the thoughtful eyes, aspired to become a scholar. Mr. Pan burnt incense in the Lion Temple in gratitude for the honour to be visited upon his house by the boy's ambition. He ordered a fine padded coat to be made for the youth, of vermilion cloth, and desired black dragons with gold tongues to be embroidered on the sleeves. On the windy morning in spring when the boy was to set out for the capital to begin his studies, Mr. Pan made him a present of a scroll and writing brushes. He put into his nephew's hand a purse in which he had placed forty pieces of silver from the chest, leaving for himself only five, and he embraced Virtue of Tranquility tenderly, exhorting him to remember the family name and bring lustre to it.

Mr. Pan stood in the gateway and watched the bright coat move down the street until crowds of many people obscured it. He turned to walk back into his garden. He saw that the red lacquer gate was marked and marred, many stalks of the bamboo were broken and lay this way and that among the green stems, the goldfish pool was empty of life, and most of the rich grass of the garden had been trampled to death, so that many patches were bare and the earth baked. From under a low-spreading leaf of the banana tree peeked a fragment of blue-and-white teacup, broken once by Little Willow Tree during the washing up.

Mr. Pan walked down the garden, and the playful wind lifted his cap from his head and dropped it into the pool, where it floated on the shallow water. He bent, picked it up, shaking the water drops from it, and without considering whether the cold and dampness might be bad for him, placed it on his head. Mr. Pan smiled. He was poorer than he had ever deemed possible; his inheritance and his own earnings were exhausted except for five silver pieces, but he was sound of body and tranquility dwelt in his breast. He looked out. He looked out beyond the city walls at the hills, which were blue as rare porcelain, with here and there the square of a field or the red dot of a house. Mr. Pan drew in a full breath of the strong spring breeze, and his nostrils expanded and he smiled once more, and the scent of plum blossoms came drifting down to him upon the fragrant wind.

#   #

GOAT SONG (6)

    March is jumpy as a jackrabbit in the Southern Oregon hill country. It'll pour down rain for two weeks, no harder, no softer, like it'll never quit, and then you'll get a week of warm weather almost as good as summer, except the creeks are up so high with water all out over the bottoms. The winter wheat's up four, five inches, that pretty light yellow-green spread wide across the valley, and the fir and pine tips are decked out with new growth.

    But it ain't the weather or stuff growing that gets you feeling so jumpy and loose-footed. It ain't the wind cutting sharp off the peaks where the snow still lays and the sun warming your back at the same time. It's something in the air, though, kind of like a question that ought to be answered, and maybe if you'd just step down the creek a piece where the willows are coming out, or up in the barn road, you could hear it plain and know for sure what it was, instead of just drifting around like you do.

    Old Rupe Gittle would never've done what he done if it hadn't come on him just at that uneasy, restless time of year. Rupe was still a pretty good man for fifty, sober and respected by all. His place laid up Butcher Knife Creek, a nice piece about sixty acres, mostly bottomland, and he owned maybe three hundred acres of fair timber up along the highway. Rupe was a good neighbor, kept his stock up in good shape, and usually gave his wife a hand with her chores when he was around the house, which is better than a good many men up this way do, but he didn't have many friends in a personal way.

    It wasn't that folks didn't care for him. He

just wasn't easy to know. He was different. Not that most men aren't different from each other. You can look through the valley and say Jake Roper here is tight-fisted, a first-rate stock man but hard on his help and stingy with the table he sets. Or you can point out old Gates, who'll set any stranger down for a good meal, but he'll mend the hole in his chicken yard fence with a piece of binder twine, provided he gets around to it, and he spends all spring figuring up what a good crop of oats he's going to take off his bench land this year but he finally never gets the seed in the ground. Men like that are as different as you'd think one man could be from another, but there's nothing strange about them. You know just how to take both of them.

    The thing about Rupe, you never knew where you were with him. For instance, we all take a turn now and then at picking a little meat out of the hills out of season. You hunt two or three days through that brush country and sleep on the rocks at night with frost coming through your blanket, and you don't get one good sight at even a forked-horn, and you'll come down sore and tired and cussing your luck. That's one way where Rupe was unnatural. He didn't care whether he come back with meat or not. He was contented either way. Half the time he'd just set around camp with no load in his gun; but he'd eat his piece of venison if anybody bring in a buck, only he never says, "Well, it's my turn to bag one tomorrow, boys," like you do when you eat somebody else's kill. You can't share the ordinary give and take with a man like that.

    I been working the forty just below Rupe's place for five years now, and I've come to know him more than most. You just take him like the weather, that it's bound to go against the signs; but when it does, it don't seem contrary to have it happening. It

Eleven Stories ... plus

just seems natural weather. That's how his way has come to seem more or less natural to me. But it would sound queer to the rest of the valley, what he told me about how he was took, there in March. It would upset their minds worse than what they think they saw. The way it is now, they think they see it clear, and most of the ladies is shocked and the men thinks it's pretty funny. But they wouldn't like any of it to be beyond them: that would anger them. As it stands, it's only Rupe's shame they feel, not their own shame.

Rupe had got his lower twenty plowed when a rain come up, and when it cleared, the land was too wet to work. His cows wasn't due to freshen for another month and chores was light. So this Friday morning he cut over across his woodlot toward the highway, thinking he'd size up his timber as he was working on a deal for him to sell off a quarter section to the mill.

He walked along easy, being in no hurry, and the moss was spongy underfoot. It was cold in the shade and sun-soaking warm in the clearings, and the air smelt clean and good from last night's rain. That's when the trees stirring begun to stir him up too, and when a jay screeched at him out of a sugar pine, he could almost make out what it was like to wear wings and screech up on a high rocking pine on a March morning.

The leaves suddenly come at him with a hundred different shapes, madrones long and glossy, cedar flat and drooping, pink curls on the oak brush, poison oak dainty shaped and shiny, and the reason for pine needles being like they are begun to bother him.

He come out on the bridge over Butcher Knife, and watching the water pouring down fast, deep and green and foaming, not like the clear shallow creek it is in summer when you can see the gravel and its different colors plain from the bridge rail, watching this restless, dark, shoving, jumping water, his fifty years stood up to him and questions bust in him that he couldn't answer.

He stopped by Ed Soles's and Ed was out in the sheep shed with an old ewe that was lambing. Rupe stood by the door and watched until it dropped, the bulging sheep heaving away and then this gangly lamb, all legs and wet wool, with big black spots around its eyes. Rupe got down on his knees by the lamb and felt it like he'd never seen one before.

"What's it for?" he asked Ed Soles.

"What's what for?" says Ed.

"What's this lamb for?"

"Why, hell," says Ed, "It's for meat."

"It ain't enough," says Rupe very slow, turning the lamb's big-eyed face up to look at it. "Look at him. He don't have to ask no questions. By Gol, Ed, he knows."

"He don't know he's gonna be meat."

"He knows something I don't," says Rupe. "And when you get down to it, what's meat for?"

"It's always been thought by most folks I know, that meat was to eat," says Ed very careful.

"All right," says Rupe "then what is folks for?"

"To eat the meat," yells Ed and busts out laughing. Rupe goes sort of slow out the door. He cut up to the timber through Ed's last year's corn patch, tromping on the black stalks. Where the logging road comes out of that burnt-over stretch he run across a hen turkey that had stolen an early nest. That shows how quick his sight for live things was that morning. You can walk right over a nesting turkey and ninety-nine times out of a hundred you won't see anything different from the brush and leaves.

Rupe stood and watched her. It was still in the trees. The dead leaves on the ground was too wet and winter-rotted to ruffle up in the wind. There wasn't a natural sound. And there sat that big bronze bird watching him with a wild look in her eye and not a feather stirring. He could tell by the look of her that she was already light and wasted by the setting fever, burning herself up to heat that clutch of big brown-speckled eggs he knew was under her. But there was a crazy joy in her, too, for all she was scared stiff of Rupe's coming near her. It come out of her like a big swell of sound in the quiet, with both of them holding dead still. You could as good as hear it. It begun like a fiddle starting slow and swelling out strong in the stillness, and it begun to sing through Rupe like some wild life in him had come alive at the sound of it, and he knew the bronze and him were kin.

    He come on down the logging road through the thick clay mud to the little log house where Hob and Beulah Cord had been spending the winter. Hob was over near Medford on a trucking job, but Beulah and the young one was there. Beulah had some wash out soaking in a tub by the door, and one of the Tremaine boys was up talking to her.

    There was always some young punk hanging around Beulah when Hob was away, and they was plenty of folks said Hob should be told for his own good. Still there wasn't anybody knew nothing definitely bad of her. She'd cut a pretty wide swath among the boys before her and Hob was married, and eighteen is pretty young for a girl full of life and good looks to be settled down steady to washing and keeping house and a two year old young one.

    Anyhow, here the two of them was, laughing and leaning on the oak tree opposite each other. Beulah was a pretty thing to see there in the sunshine. You could tell from the way she swung her legs or stretched out an arm high and easy, like a cat humping itself slow just to enjoy the feeling, how young she was and how she liked being how she was and where she was just that minute.

You get older and you don't move like that, just for the joy of that slick lazy feeling in your muscles. You know just where the twinge'll catch you in your shoulder. You got to make up your mind to get up on your legs and get them going along until such time as you can set down and give them a rest. You forget what the feel of your own swinging young body was like.

There was Beulah, plump and pretty and every bit of her just burning with life. It was some ways like the lamb getting its first sight of the world, or the turkey hen blazing her life near out over them eggs, but it was even better and more human. If human beings are works of art, Beulah was a prime piece of creation, not in any way warped or spoiled. Her buttocks was soft and plump and showed under her dress like two loaves of light bread, raised high and ready for the oven. One of them would tighten up and then slip down as her foot swung, and it was a good and enjoyable sight. She was a fine thing, made for living, and doing what she was made for, not spoiling a minute of her young time by thinking about it, just a sweet young female drawing the young males to her like a pranksome young doe draws the bucks around in mating month.

Rupe stood in the road watching her, the blood spouting through him like swift water through a flume, and his heart shouting with the same joy as if he's the Lord that made her the pretty thing she was, until she felt somebody looking at her and turned around and went grown up and proper, and says, "Good morning, Mr. Gittle."

Rupe says, "Good morning, Miz Cord; morning, Tremaine," and walks on by.

All day he wanders around aimless, through pastures and up over timber land, seeking an answer for what he don't know. And the more he walks, the more he sees the dumb things know, but they give him no answer.

When late afternoon come, he went home and did what milking there was, and after he'd separated and washed up, he come into the kitchen and watched his wife setting supper on the table. There was buttered hominy and thick fried ham with milk gravy and baked potatoes and home-canned peas and bread and fresh butter and raspberry jam and sweet pickles and two fat pies. And all this seemed better than good to him, like it had some fine meaning too. And his wife seemed better than ordinary; burnt out and scraggly as she might be, the age was natural on her, like a scraggly redwood, still hardy after a forest fire's left it.

"Wife," he says, "a woman oftentimes has more knowledge than you'd expect, so I'll ask you the question that's plaguing me. What can a man do to make his years count to him?"

"I'll tell you what a man can do, Rupe Gittle," his wife tells him. "If he's worth his salt he don't go roaming the countryside all day and leave his good dinner spoil on the stove and his wife with a full day's work and all the chores extra. Look at that woodbox," she says, "and you'll see something you could tend to." She's a good woman but she has a puckered tongue.

Rupe sits down to the table and eats a hearty meal. Then he goes out and brings in two armloads of stovewood and splits up kindling for the morning fires. But after the wood's in, he takes his hat and goes out again. And he don't come home until four in the morning and when he comes he's got a lump on his head as big as a turkey egg.

It all come out that next morning down to Carl Erblacher's store, and by noon everybody up and down Butcher Knife Creek was laughing about it. Beulah Cord tells Miz Erblacher, and that's the quickest way to spread a story around here that there is, how the old rooster come to her place in the dead of night and wants to be let in. Folks may talk about Beulah, but she sure knows what she don't want, and when Rupe won't take no for an answer but keeps demanding to come in, she reaches out the window and fetches him one on the head with a stick of stovewood.

There is a water meeting that night and Rupe is on the Board, and there's a lot of small betting as to whether he shows up or not. You never seen a bigger crowd turn out for water meeting. Everybody was there and all the young ones racing around out in the schoolyard and falling out of trees and raising a hullabaloo. But sure enough, along about eight o'clock up drives Rupe and Miz Gittle in their old car.

Ham Splicer's the first one to sing out. All the Splicers talks a good bit faster than they can think. "Give us the straight of it, Rupe," he yells. "These gals that don't take it easy are hell, ain't they?"

Rupe looks at him kind of gentle, like you would to a frisky calf that was butting around too much.

"You boys got it all wrong," he says.

He gets out of the car and he seems like he thinks he's got to explain something. He looks at Ham Splicer and Johnny Gates.

"It's something I've been looking for," he says. "Things have got it, and some folks have got it but they don't appear to know it. It's a kind of brightness," he says, "like flume water washing down strong. I never seen it before yesterday," he says, "and I never seen it before in a human. Folks could see it," he says, "if their eyes wasn't so fog thick with common matters. Only they don't know where to look for it."

"You ain't the only one that's looked for it up at that place," says Charlie Soles, and the crowd laughs.

Rupe looks perplexed. "It don't seem like I can explain it," he says.

"You don't have to, you old goat!" yips Ham Splicer again, and then Miz Gittle takes Rupe's arm and pushes him in to the meeting.

Miz Gittle stood by Rupe fine, though what she may have had to say at home I would of like to have heard. Rupe took a lot of talk for the next couple of weeks, but then a warm wind come up that dried the land so it was right for plowing, and the spring work got underway.

The talk just kind of died out, and Rupe must of forgot most of it too. You got no more time to go roaming the woods after any young does when the soil's scouring smooth off the plow blade and crumbling back from the furrow, and harrowing and floating and drilling ahead and the incubators full and ten cows coming in, one after another, with the milking running heavy and the calves to feed, and garden to put in. A farmer's got too much close at hand to keep him occupied, in April.

# #

Kressmann Taylor

Girl in a Blue Rayon Dress (7)

    It was a fear in Ellie Pearl that the scent of
the trees was so sweet and strong in the first dark,
with wet-dirt smell and pine pitch and needle smell,
like when she was knee high and ran barefoot and knew
every trail in these parts, pine land or granite, able
to run quick and true without counting where she laid
her foot. It came back too strong now, she treading up
the steep last stretch through woodland, treading pine
needles dry and slick, sliding her in her town shoes
with their smooth leather bottoms. Cricket's song was
loud for company, with the trees so black and thick
that through the cracks in the woods, the night sky
looked lightened. A little hoot owl hooted up on the
mountain, and the sound trembled down to Ellie Pearl
like a fear. It was a safe sound, a scared, safe sound,
like the trees moving a little in the dark.
    She said, "Give me room now please; give me
time. Don't hurry me. Because I didn't expect to be so
acquainted again, not all at once."
    When she came to the creek where the log went
over, she had to stand and listen to the water rushing.
It kept coming down and coming down like this
all the time out of nowhere up in the mountain, and
going away down valley, where she had never seen where
it went. She had to squat down and feel out for the
log with her hand, the water was so black dark. She
felt the top of the log where the wood was some rotted
and broke loose in light chunks, and, after, the
underside, bristly with moss and damp. She thought how
she would surely catch the heels of her shoes and fall
if she walked across, and felt of her dress that was
blue rayon and brittle as paper and had cut-glass
buttons that sparkled in the light of day, and she

couldn't think what she would do if she wet it. It was a strange thought that she didn't care so much whether she wet it or not, here in the woods with all the smells and sounds of the night. Finally she took off her shoes and stockings and held them in one hand and her suitcase in the other, and went out on the log and felt crumbly wood under her bare feet. The noise of the water came from no direction, and halfway over she was tipsy in space and had to bend down and find the log in front of her by feeling, and her stockings caught on the wood and she thought probably she had torn them, and there was a feel of cold air from the moving of the creek water, on her face, and the smell of wood rot from the log. She went half stooped over, feeling ahead with her feet.

  Where the log ended she jumped down into high grass and sat, and the seedheads rasped her elbows as she put her shoes and stockings on again because of how she wanted them to see her when she came to the house. It was a funny feeling, sitting there and feeling along her skin for her garters in the dark. For a minute she didn't know who on earth she was, and the five miles back down mountain to the paved road, where she had left the bus, were clear, every step, dirt trail and rock slab, cedar and madrone and huckleberry thicket; but the bus was like she had only dreamed it. And still, where she had come from she didn't know, although only this morning the office where her typewriter sat over in the corner by the window that looked out on the Crossroads Diner had seemed nice and the only real place in the world. And Mr. Brian from the sales force, always touching her elbow when she sat down to take dictation. He had taken her to the movies six times and had told her about his savings account, and had kissed her respectfully, after the second time. And now, he was like somebody she had dreamed once somewhere and she was tying her shoes and rising stiffly to her feet in the thick grass and moving ahead into the resinous air of pine woods once more.

She must have gone off the path somewhere in the pines, for when sky broke through ahead she was at the high edge of the woods, and there was the old rail fence that bounded the lower pasture, set here and there with boulders that whitened in the starlight; and she laid down a rail and climbed across, minding her dress, and plodded clumsily along the rough ground until she saw the loom of the oak trees that shaded the house and the sudden lighted square of the kitchen window.

Mama was flouring down a big round of dough in the bread bowl on the table. And Grandma in her rocking chair, her head dropped over, traveled away somewhere in sleep, a little light-weight woman, her nose and mouth drawn close together like a cat's in her shriveled face. The lamp was one spot of brightness in its bracket up on the wall. And Papa and Ruby sat in chairs by the stove, Ruby with her hair put up and reading the catalogue, the wishing book, the way the two of them both used to together, and Papa stooped and tired with his hard thick hands at rest on his knees.

Mama said, "Ellie Pearl!"

Nobody knew much to say, and Ellie Pearl opened her suitcase on the floor and gave out their presents one at a time. She had gotten Mama a bottle of violet perfume, and Papa a one-pound can of Velvet tobacco. For Ruby she had a ring with a blue middle stone with a little hoop of glass diamonds running around the edge. The ring fitted Ruby's middle finger, and Ruby liked it there, and Ellie Pearl felt a wide sad distance spreading between her and her sister, because Ellie Pearl had learned, living in the town, what finger a ring ought to be worn on. For Grandma she had bought a square silk scarf with bunches of blue roses on it, that had cost a dollar. She had presents for the others, too, but her brother True was down to the Grange to a dance, and the other children had gone to bed already. She missed seeing them tonight, because she had just one week's vacation and then she would go back again.

In the morning she put on her old red dress that she had left here in the clothes closet last year, and her old flat mountain shoes. Ellie Pearl took the water bucket and went out to the pump; and out under the oak trees, the morning coldness and the clean smell of the air surprised her. It surprised her that she had forgotten what it was like to go outdoors in the morning, with the sky paling and losing grayness over in the east. She primed the pump from the can and began to work the iron handle with her strangely unused arms, but she hadn't got the water up yet when a big brown hand out of a blue shirt sleeve took hold of the handle, and she let go, and True did the pumping for her in strong man-style.

True said, "You going back again?"

"Of course" she said. "I finished the typing course and I work for Goldring and Sons, and I've saved twenty dollars. When I've saved fifty, I'm going to take the course in bookkeeping."

True said without emphasis, "Tige Tigard had Margaret Walton with him to the dance last night."

"Well, let him." Ellie Pearl said and thought how the mornings were pretty cold up here in the mountains, and put Tige Tigard aside.

Mama said, "I'm glad one of my children had enough get-up-and-go to her to take herself out of these hills." Papa didn't say a word. "A man don't know." Mama said. "Hoein', bakin', scrubbin', washin', cookin', from dawn till dark." Mama had eight children, but she was lean and her stomach never got baggy and big like some lazy woman's.

Ellie Pearl crouched on the soft earth of the garden under the noon sun. The sun was hot and the weeds smelt dusty. Mama made too much fuss, she decided, about her Ellie Pearl's job and about how her Ellie Pearl had made up her mind and gone away and done so well for herself. She made it almost so Ellie Pearl couldn't come home and feel at home, and her little brothers, Henry and Loyal, and baby Sophia had been made to act embarrassed and didn't make up to her. Mama had no call to act that way. It wasn't as if Mama had done it, although Mama had always pushed her on and encouraged. She, Ellie Pearl had made up her own mind, as soon as she saw that she could do good in school. She'd worked and paid for it all, too. And now she had nice clothes, and she and another girl where she lived shared a bathroom with a looking glass and a white bathtub. And Mr. Brian had told her that when he got married, his wife wouldn't have to get her pretty hands rough and red because he was going to have a dishwasher installed and other labor-saving devices.

Late on that Sunday afternoon (Ellie Pearl had come home on Saturday), an old car came bouncing and jolting along the ruts in the dirt road, and it was Ellie Pearl's two married brothers come over to see her and bringing along their wives and a jug of cider. They all sat out on the porch, and Ellie Pearl learned the major events that had happened during her year of separation.

True told how in April Tige Tigard had shot him a mountain lion and had the skin tanned for a rug. He didn't look at Ellie Pearl but it was her he told it for. Mama called them all in to supper, and there she and Ruby had made cake and had turned a freezer of ice cream. When Ellie Pearl tasted the first spoon of ice cream, all of a sudden that taste made her so homesick to be a little girl again that she wanted to cry her grief, for what was lost, lost to time, and never could be gotten back.

It wasn't till Tuesday that Tige Tigard came by, and then it was to return a horse collar he'd had to borrow. It wasn't like Tige Tigard to care enough about farming to bother borrowing a horse collar; it was surprising. Tige would always rather hunt up in the hills. And Ellie Pearl had forgotten until she saw him come riding into the yard, how big he was. There he was, getting down from his horse, a big tall, broad-shouldered man with longish dark hair slicked back, and with a firm mouth in his sun-browned face, and a hunter's eyes, always looking off over the edge of the world. Two years ago Tige Tigard had paid down on his land, a high piece up near the pass, about twenty acres of mountain meadow with a good stream running through and a considerable piece of virgin timber along with it. The house on it wasn't much more than a shack, but Tige had built a porch on the front, where he could sit with his feet on the rail and look off down the valley.

Tige Tigard had on a clean blue workshirt and wore a hunting knife. He stood alongside of Ellie Pearl in the yard for a while without speaking. Then he asked Ellie Pearl if he could take her to the dance on Saturday night.

Ellie Pearl felt pleased to know that Margaret Walton didn't have him all tied up, because she felt Margaret was a girl who didn't show much promise, at least not for a man like Tige.

"I'd be pleased to attend the dance in your company, Tige Tigard." Ellie Pearl told him.

Tige Tigard looked down at her through squinted eyes, and she fairly had to look up at him. "You're talkin' pretty fancy, ain't you, Ellie Pearl?" he asked her, and there were little lights in his eyes like a smile.

"I see no reason why I can't talk nice if I know how, Tige Tigard," she answered him, and she didn't know why she was so vexed and discontented.

Ellie Pearl was fretting more than she ought to have, being at home and nothing happening to unsettle her. Sometimes everything was easy and long-accustomed and she was purely happy, like scouring up the old tin pans to make them shine and smelling the fresh bread out of the oven. But sometimes, especially when she walked up-mountain onto the granite, where she had loved the outlook best ever since she was small, she would sit down on the hard rock, ridged white rock with its little granular markings of gold and of black, so beautiful it was the pick of all rock, and watch the little lizards scuttle and run and the sky one sheet of plain blue over her head, and all the joy of it was sunken and lost and she just ached and hankered inside and she didn't know what for.

On Friday morning she mentioned the trouble to her grandma, after she had set a chair for the tiny old lady and settled her out in the oak shade in the side yard with her Bible in her lap. Grandma paid a lot too much mind to the Bible and got too much misery out of it, Ellie Pearl sometimes thought; but there was just no use talking to Mama, who had her fixed notions and didn't look beyond them, or to True, who was contented like he was, without thinking about things. And Ruby was too young and wanting. Ellie Pearl sat herself down in the deep green grass, cool and kind against her bare legs. "Grandma, what's the matter with me? I ought to be happy, being here and I'm just perfectly miserable."

Her grandma's puckered little face wavered and then steadied on her. "You bought your pretties, child, and you're paying the price, paying the price," she pronounced. "As ye sow, so shall ye reap," Grandma said. "I sowed the wind when I was young, and I've reaped the whirlwind all my years, in dust and ashes. In dust and ashes."

"Do you mean when you and Grandpa were burnt out?" Ellie Pearl asked.

"What you yearn for and cling to dries in the hand," Grandma said, and her old hands twisted together in a wringing motion. "Make your bargain with the Lord, and your punishment is that what you get is what you asked for."

"But I know what I want," Ellie Pearl tried to tell her. "I'm happy about everything I've done. Only I'm just not happy," she said lamely.

"I chose the things of this world," the old voice droned on, far away in the past. "I could have had my joy, but I chose the things of this world. The kingdom of heaven is a pearl of great price," she whined in her thin preaching voice. "Sell all that you have and buy it." Her little head drowsed on her neck.

On Saturday, the morning of the dance night, Ellie Pearl put up her yellow hair in the aluminum curlers she had bought in the five-and-dime. Then she laid out the silver evening bag and put a handkerchief in it.

Tige Tigard came for her in a car. It wasn't his, but he had borrowed it. He let her get in by herself, and didn't drive her straight to the dance. He took them around a back road to Eagle Rock, and there he stopped and they got out. She didn't want to sit down on a rock because of her dress, but Tige sat down on a low boulder with his legs stretched out in front of him. He had on new Levi's and a red plaid shirt, and his forearms were big and solid and bare. There was a half moon high in the sky, and she could see him plain, and the white granite above them and down below a stretch of pine woods running away like water under the moonlight.

"I painted my house," Tige said.

"You did?" she said. "What color?"

"Well, red," Tige answered, and that made him angry. "Red barn paint. You don't think I could afford house paint at six dollars a gallon?"

She shouldn't have said that, and she looked around for something to say. "That's a fine pair of boots you've got on," she said, and they were fine, coming clear up to the knee and very supple and beautiful.

"Handmade," he said, "Thirty-five dollars."
And that got him even madder than before. "Oh, you" he shouted, 'You don't know anything!"

Ellie Pearl felt terrible because they were quarreling already and because she had belittled him to himself. She walked away a few steps down the road. Then she just stood still and waited. There was a sound somewhere in the night, distant, high and strange.

"Listen," she said, and Tige had heard it and was looking up. In a minute Tige saw it and pointed, but she couldn't find it; and he came over to her and turned her head up more to the north, and there they were, dark against the light, a vast V of wild ducks traveling south, outlined in air below the moon. And as they streamed out, their continuous high chatter floated down like muted talk to the two on the ground there, out of the sky. And as the thin lines faded in moonlight off to the south, and the girl and the man began to steady a little, there was again the high hooting palaver in the air, and another great V, and still another, trailing half along the sky. They two stood very close together and without speaking watched them fade south across the zenith, until the last lean echo died.

"Early," Tige said at last. "There'll be early frosts in the fall."

"How can they tell?" Ellie Pearl said painfully but insistently.

"They've got to," Tige answered her coldly. "It's a need." He stopped because a shame took him to put things into talk. Ellie Pearl looked up into the whitish sky. She put her manicured white hands on Tige Tigard's forearm holding her, and the long corded muscles were solid ropes under the brown skin, and she wavered but hung on to his silent hardness.

Then Tige Tigard just moved and swung her, his hand holding her against her ribs. He put his other big hand on the back of her head and pressed her mouth hard to his mouth. His body in the red plaid shirt and the stiff Levi's was firm and alive against her and he bent her slowly back and forth, his shoulders swaying like a tree wagging in the wind. He smelled like whiskey and apples, and Ellie Pearl swung like the earth in its orbit under the pressure of the man and the mountains and the night. O, Tige Tigard; O, hold hard and sweet! Natural soft noises of the earth thrummed out a chorus in the ears of the two of them clinging there. It came gently to Ellie Pearl that the twenty dollars would buy a sow to start them raising pigs for next year's ham and bacon, to hang in the cellar of their red house with the lion-skin rug, up there in the mountain meadow among the peaks.

#   #   #

The Pale Green Fishes (8)

It was full summer when Charles Corey came home from a week's selling trip, on a scented, burnished afternoon of goldenrod and gentle airs that was very pleasant to walk in, after the cindered heat of local trains, the icy air-conditioning of hotel lobbies and barrooms. When he reached his house and came down the graveled pathway from the gate, he saw his wife at work, and his younger son with her, amidst the greenery of the side garden with its masses of rosy phlox and crimson hibiscus, the river gleaming darkly in long glints and streaks through the shadowy willow trees beyond their heads.

He noted that she had chosen to work in the flowers, and not in the vegetable garden, where he would have preferred to find her, but his mind made the reflection without animosity. He even had a pleasant sense of forgiving her for a minor neglect of duty, because this was his day of return, and these weekly homecomings were always fraught for him with an almost moist-eyed tenderness (he felt the glow of it within himself now), a desire to enwrap, to embrace this little family circle that he ruled, that he had made, to close them to himself, to shut out the world.

As the gravel grated under his shoes he watched his wife, still busily working, still unaware of him, and the sight of her compact, golden body in the sunlight, her rather heavy thighs and freckled shoulders emerging from the faded calico-red shorts and halter she wore, sent a sharp sting of possessive satisfaction through him.

The boy saw him first and broke away from his work, leaping toward the man with his awkward nine-year-old gait, and flung himself convulsively at his father's knees.

Charles Corey held his son off, somewhat impatiently. "All right, all right, you little son of a gun. Give me a chance to kiss your mother first, will you?"

He handed the boy his heavy briefcase, and the youngster turned and went loping ahead of him, his right shoulder sagging importantly with the weight. Mary Corey stood up and wiped the hair back from her forehead with her bare arm. Her look changed from serenity to a slow pleasure of welcome, a brightness that touched all the lines of her body and quickened her small fragile face to vividness. She came towards him, moving quickly, a garden trowel in her hand.

"Don't get that damned thing on my clothes," he said and reached down for her mouth, kissing her slowly, his lips moist and probing, while she lay against him happily, and the boy, Richard, watched them absorbedly, his young eyes showing his contentment at having them together like this. Now it would begin, the boy knew, that fine first day, and he was full of eagerness as they began to walk to the house, his father holding his mother to his side, while she held the garden trowel away from them with her free hand.

And, as always, his father went first to pull the shades down, for he liked the rooms dark and cool in summer. His mother always kept windows and blinds open, letting the sun play in little flickering hot lights over the dark woodwork, underlighting the warm glow of the Turkey-red curtains, the late afternoon sun throwing its ruddy spangles, its languid beams, through the deepness of the room. But when his father pulled the blinds down close, there was a still, bloody darkness, a stale hush of air, as if the house had closed inexorably around them in a hot, binding silence and red-brown dusk, and they could never,

never get out.

    But it was in that strange ruddy twilight that everything began. His mother would bring in two glasses of beer with foam piling on the top as if it were going to spill over, and tiny bright bubbles that kept climbing up and up the glass. The liquid looked a rich brown color, although Richard knew that in the light it would be golden. And sure enough, after his father had taken a deep drink, so deep that you could see how it satisfied him, and had wiped the edges of his mustache with his folded handkerchief, his voice began to rise to that fine tone of importance, and he began to tell them everything, bringing the unknown world of busy cities and bustling crowds, the strange places, the men with wonderful names, that his father knew, into their own house, into the red-brown hush with them. And his mother sat smiling and smiling with pleasure, and now and then sipped carefully at her beer, testing it, as if it were something bitter that she discovered each time, but that still pleased her with its taste. And his father talked.

    His father knew all about everything. His mother did not know so very much. She was always asking herself questions. She couldn't understand why some leaves, like the willows, grew so long and thin, while others were finger-edged and flat. She was always tasting, sniffing, feeling things with her hands--bark and little stones and fur and the smooth of dishes. If you watched you could catch her at it, and she would grow a little shy and embarrassed; but the boy could see very well why she was obliged to do it. He himself could not get enough of the cool resistance of the river water when he ran his hands through it, or of the springy separate blades of the grass against his bare toes. His mother was not quite adult. She was always testing the world in her slow, pleased way. She was always wondering at it. But his father knew it. His father knew, surely, all about everything.

It was wonderful to hear him talking now, his voice so exultant and alive, and his mother marveling at him. The boy's heart glowed with joy for this fineness, with his mother sitting beside him, both of them receiving, silent and intent, this drinking in of marvels that the rich voice gave them. Even the men with the important names had to stop, to listen, to recognize the wonder of his father.

His father crossed his knees and lighted a cigar, and the tip glowed rosy and round in the dimness and depth of the room, while the sweet strong scent smote their nostrils.

"I gave it to him absolutely straight," he said, his voice throbbing with masculine exultancy. "I told him, 'Look here, J.F., do you want me to lay it on the line for you?' And then I gave it to him. Gave it to him straight from the shoulder. And he couldn't say a word. He knew I had him. My God, Mary, I wish you could have seen the big blusterer's face."

The boy knew that "J.F." was president of his father's company, and he could see the whole scene as his father painted it, this "J.F." with a white face, cowed and waiting, while his father stood proudly over him and "laid it on the line." The very words were wonderful, and the boy marveled as he was bidden at the pride, the handsomeness, the splendid sureness of his father. A proudness shone from the man, from the taut cream-colored fabric of his summer suit buttoned around his heavy girth, from the thick curl of hair that flowed back in assurance from his high forehead.

Richard's face flushed and he looked at his mother. But her eyes had suddenly lost their happiness, although her mouth still smiled loosely. She was going to say something. She was going to spoil it all. He

Eleven Stories ... plus

hated her.

But his mother did not speak, and his father went on talking, and gradually the warmth came back into the boy, while, surreptitiously, he watched his mother's face begin to brighten, to receive his father again.

"The political situation..." his father was saying, and a moment later, "credit situation..."; and the words "political situation, credit situation" as he spoke them had a distant thunder in them, an ominous hugeness. The hugeness and dark roar of them swelled and began to occupy and lurk in the far corners of the room; for this rosy darkness was a wonderful thing, and if the boy gave himself to it, lost himself in it, he could evoke jinn in its distant corners. Now he made out a spiral there, something heavy and dark that moved and curled and waited, over there where the dining-room door should be; something unquiet that kept changing its shape in the same way the masses of summer clouds, which looked so still until you really watched them, billowed and frayed and changed. You could discover a monstrous head, and before your eyes had even caught it, the long fangs shredded away into vapor and the shape writhed and became the crude, stretching body of an animal. His father's words sounded on his outer ear: "... they're covering it up. I got it absolutely straight from Jim Regan, down in Washington." And the deep, portentous tone of the words intensified for the boy the menace, the overwhelming swirl of darkness and thunder and danger in the corner there.

The thin trail of cigar smoke that floated in a brownish plane above their heads rolled almost imperceptibly, in the still air, closer and closer to the end of the room, to the edge of that dangerous coiling dusk. The boy watched in tremulous fascination until the first tentacles of smoke touched and entered the gloom, and he was no longer listening but was absorbed, rapt, half afraid and half excited, on the near side of those brown and thickening shadows that sucked in and ate the faint smoke.

Always this menace lurked behind the pleasant everyday world; everywhere there were these dark and shapeless powers that reached silently out of corners, out of shadows, out of night, searching for him, shaking him, luring him, almost against his will, closer and closer to the edge of dark and nebulous chaos. The waiting evil spread its brown smoke tentacles in the hot and silent darkness, and dreading it, desiring it, all his senses attuned to the thin danger of it, he began to float like smoke, was drawn, was sucked nearer, nearer. . ..

Silence in the room broke him out of his absorption, and he saw his mother's eyes fastened on him in troubled warning. He said, "Yes, sir,," quickly, automatically, aware with a pang that his father had spoken to him, but unable to hear the words, which had touched only his outer ear and floated now somewhere in his mind like an echo, just out of reach. He tried to meet his father's eyes boldly.

"Dreaming again," his father said contemptuously, and he answered, "Yes, sir. I'm sorry," very quickly. "I asked you how you were doing in school" the man's voice told him.

"Oh -- all right," he said, "All right, I think,"

"You think?" his father demanded coldly. "Don't you know?"

"Yes, sir," he said. I'm doing all right."

His throat was immediately full of a choking closeness, and he felt sick as if he were going to throw up, because his father's face had grown hard and punishing, and the fineness of the day was broken, and

Eleven Stories ... plus

it was he, Richard, who had done it. In despair he watched his father turn the hard look on his mother.

"Give the boy time enough alone with you and you'll make a woman of him yet. That's what you'd like, isn't it?" he said bitterly.

Then Richard saw that his mother was going to save them. Her face did not grow hushed, turned inward, flinching, as it usually did when his father spoke to her like that. Her eyes remained merry, and she pursed her lips in a pretty pout and laughed, and his father's face grew red and pleased, and he pulled Mother close against him and covered her lips with a slow long-held kiss. Only, his mother no longer relaxed in the embrace, as in the garden. She held her mouth up to the kiss, but her shoulders were curled and tight, and her hands were two small fists at her sides instead of spreading out happily on his father's back. She had saved them but she was ashamed; and was suffering for it. But the boy, clinging wildly to the remnants of the magical day--still safe, still going on--was too relieved to care.

They had dinner on the screened porch that looked out over the river, the three of them. His older brother, Gordon, was spending two weeks at Scout camp, and his father had not yet mentioned him. There was cold watermelon, and Richard was very careful not to spit the seeds, glancing hopefully at his father from time to time to see whether he observed how well his young son was eating. But his father was not caring, yet, how they behaved. All that would come tomorrow.

He was still full of exuberance and talk, and when they had finished eating, he leaned back and sighed, and then called Mother over and made her sit down on his knees and caught her arms in his hands and bent his head a little, and said suddenly in a low voice, half impelling, half pleading, "You do believe in me, don't you, Mary?" His mother's head lifted quickly and her face lightened, and she put up one hand and touched his hair. Then his hands gripped her arms tightly and he pressed his head down against her bosom and said, "Please believe in me. Please love me."

His mother murmured in a sort of singing tone, only shyly, "All right," and her face was very lovely, and she was smiling.

His father lifted his head and ran his hands over Mother's shoulders and up into her hair, and he said to her, "You have a little brown mole on your neck, just under your left ear," and they both laughed, and his mother was very happy again. Up the river the sun was going down in a red haze behind the mountain, and their faces were flushed with its pink reflection, and on the table the plates lay in a shining triangle, full of rosy pools of watermelon juice, and the smell of coolness came up to them from the river, and everything was wonderful.

The morning light came white and thin, with a low mist screening the river and the feeling of heat already strong in the day. The boy slid hurriedly out of bed, hearing noises from downstairs, a clinking of dishes, the closing of the refrigerator door, and voices in the kitchen. The fragrance of toasting bread came floating up the stairs, and the hot iron smell of the frying pan.

In the shower stall he stood flat against the side and turned the handles carefully--because the water usually came either too hot or too cold--and then edged his body into the pelting spray. He was never really dirty because he was in and out of the river so much. A stripe of white skin stretched around his loins in bright contrast to his brown legs and brown belly. He remembered that his mother had said he was painted in three sections, now that he lived all day

Eleven Stories ... plus

in his swimming trunks. Without curiosity he tested, by means of soap and shower brush, the indelibility of the hue on his thighs--the browning was an inexplicable gift from the sun, a summer change in himself. It pleased him but at the same time it baffled him that the elements could so work on him, could reach down from the far spaces around the sun and mark him thus, without his will. He lifted his head and thrust it under the full force of the shower, letting the water wash through his hair and dribble pleasantly over his face and his closed eyes.

Dressed, and with the front of his hair carefully combed where he could see it in the mirror, he made for the stairs; and before he remembered, he took a kangaroo leap down the three steps to the landing, his stiff Sunday shoes banging against the bare wood, jolting him and sending a tremor up his legs to his knees. The voices in the kitchen stopped. Then his mother's voice called quickly, a shade too lightly:

"Try to come down a little more quietly, Riccy." His father's voice, stern and peremptory, cut across her sentence. "Dick! Do you hear me?"

"Yes, sir," the boy answered, standing still on the landing, waiting and holding his breath for what he knew was coming.

"Turn around where you are." His father's voice was cold and contained. "Go back up the stairs, and then walk down them. Are you able to understand what that means? I said *walk*. Do you think you can do it?"

"Yes, sir," he called miserably and tiptoed to the top again, where he turned and, half resentful, began a cautious descent, slowly, with bent knees, and apprehensively because his leather heels made a clopping sound on each step.

He crossed the kitchen to the breakfast table and stood very stiffly before his father, whose proud, offended eyes looked him up and down.

"Good morning, sir."

His father made an impatient noise. "May I ask whether this is your usual way of coming down the stairs to breakfast?" His face was set and heavy. There was always this foreboding morning heaviness about his father.

"No, sir."

His father leaned back in his chair and his elbows moved the red-checkered breakfast cloth on the table, so that the silver clinked together. "During the week, while I am not here, you come down the stairs quietly, without this unholy clatter and racket?"

"Yes, sir," he said unhappily, his throat closing rebelliously, because lots of times he did walk down.

"I see. You mean that the only time you go crashing and battering your way around this house like some kind of mountain goat is when I am home? You do it for my benefit? Is that what you mean?"

"No, sir. I mean--" He stopped, cornered. His father's eyes were cold and demanding, forcing him to answer when he would not.

"Go on. What do you mean?"

"I'm sorry. I forgot."

The corners of his father's mouth moved slightly, and there was just a trace in them of a cool, self-satisfied smile. Now his face grew less harsh, more conciliatory, a father talking things over reasonably and honestly with his son.

"Tell me, now, isn't it true that sometimes, during the week when I am not here, you go jumping down the stairs?"

Richard relaxed his guard. "Sometimes."

"All right." The man's eyes suddenly glinted. "I thought we'd get at it eventually. So sometimes you go crashing around, beating up the house, when I am away. Is that right?" The voice was laden with justice, so

Eleven Stories ... plus

much in the right, so strong.

"Yes, sir."

His father's face grew icy. "And what does your mother say when you start tearing the place down? Be honest, now. Just exactly what does she say?"

The boy's whole mind was in struggle. He had sensed that this was coming, but he never knew how to avoid it. "She tells me not to."

"Oh, she tells you not to, does she? I wonder--just how does she go about telling you not to? What does she say? Come on, speak up."

The boy wanted frantically to run and hide his head against his mother. But he had to stand there. He could not think what to say.

His father's voice grew steely. "What's the matter with you? Can't you answer a simple question?"

"Please, Charles," his mother said very low, from where she stood by the stove, all the brightness drained from her face.

"Keep out of this," his father said fiercely, without turning his head. "This is between the boy and me. We'll see if he can give an honest answer to a simple question. Now tell me," he said stonily to the boy, weighting every word with authority, "just what your mother says to you when you jump. Does she scold you?"

"Sometimes," the boy cried, seizing on the desperate truth, giving up under the pressure of his father's fierceness. But it was terrible. It was just what he should not have said.

"Sometimes!" his father exclaimed triumphantly. "I thought so. And that means that most of the time she lets you go crashing and bulling your way around here without interfering, without even trying to stop you. Isn't that so? Isn't it?"

"Sometimes she stops me," the boy cried. He began to weep.

The man turned a blazing, injured face toward his wife. "Do you see what you're doing to the boy?" he demanded. "Look at him. Absolutely undisciplined, making a wreck out of the few sticks I manage to scrape together to cover our heads with. How can I afford to keep a decent place for us to live in when you don't care anything about it? You'd let the whole place go to pieces, wouldn't you?"

His mother's eyes were hot with anger in her pale face. Her lips moved. "That's not fair," she said tightly, almost inaudibly.

"What's that?" his father cried sharply.

His mother turned with a little gasp of fury, and saw Richard shrinking there between them. The anger slowly drained from her face, and she gave a quick little toss of the head as if to free herself of something.

"I do believe in a certain amount of discipline, Charles," she said firmly, and then before his father could answer, she came swiftly to the table with a coffee cup and a blue platter on which ham curled pinkly and the shining eggs sent up a steam from their yellow centers. "Come on and eat, you two, before everything gets cold," she said.

Richard could see that the danger was not yet over. Something dark hung and balanced in the air about his father. The big man took an impatient gulp of coffee, set the cup down hard, and then turned back to it, lifted it again and drank more slowly. "Not bad coffee, for a change," he said, and Mother gave a quick little laugh designed to make things better, and his father turned his eyes on her, not pleased but no longer angry, ready to wait, and then he picked up his knife and fork and began to eat rapidly, chewing heavily and enjoying it.

Richard eased himself into his chair. Sunlight had started to stream thinly through the outside mists and

Eleven Stories ... plus

to filter through the window curtains, a pallid white sunlight on the bright red cloth and the blue breakfast crockery. Everything in the house tingled and waited, as it always did when his father came home. Richard felt a curious hollowness in the region of his stomach, but it was not altogether the emptiness of hunger; it was partly discomfort for the scene just ended and partly a stirring apprehension and excitement for what the day would bring. There was something about his father that made things happen; the weekends were always crowded with the imminence of catastrophic event. It was like floating in the air over a bright valley crossed by erratic thunderstorms. His father kept them all moving through the hours with a high, sure vigor, but you never knew when you would unwittingly come too close to the edge of boiling cloud and find yourself shaken, lightning-struck with thunder growling through the sky.

 The long deliberateness of Sunday breakfast protracted itself almost unbearably. They ate silently except for the light ting-ing of knives and forks against the plates--his father did not encourage conversation at table--waiting for his father to announce the program for the day. Only, today everything was queer. It was because Gordon was not there and the family arrangement was all lopsided. His father could have spoken to Gordon, and the strain would have been eased. They were close together, Gordon and his father. But this Sunday morning his father was all alone, reaching for the extra ham and eggs, eating ponderously, his displeasure deliberately suspended over them. If Gordon had been there his father might have ended the trouble by making a joke about it, and Gordon would have laughed, and his father would have been satisfied. But now the strain was still there, and time kept drawing out and everything was queer.

Then his father did an extraordinary thing. He laid down his knife and fork, wiped his mouth carefully with his napkin, and turned to Richard a face that seemed to have forgotten all his indignation. "Well, son," he said, "how about you giving me a hand today, when we get back from church? I've got to fix that broken ladder, and I want to put a new spring on the screen door. Do you think you can handle a hammer without beating your thumbs to pieces?"

"Sure," Richard said excitedly, grinning. "I mean, 'Yes, sir.'"

"Well, we'll give it a try," his father said, smiling. "Maybe it's about time for you to start living in a man's world."

When they got up from the table, he clapped his hand on Richard's shoulder companionably and walked with him out on the porch, but Richard noticed that he hadn't spoken to Mother, nor looked at her yet, and it gave him a sort of empty feeling inside, in spite of the excitement of having his father notice him, because usually when things were bad, they two were left together, and that way they could rather encourage each other and not mind it too much.

Today his mother behaved very well in church, not turning her head once to look at the stained-glass window that she liked, where the light came blazing through, red as satin, but keeping her eyes steadily on the minister, her face all peaceful and cool. Richard looked at her once to see whether she was suffering, but she was not. She was not happy, either; she was just herself. And that was all right, and Richard, too, was able to behave very well, hardly wriggling at all, so that his father had to nudge him only twice. His father sang very loudly on the hymns, "Wash me, and I shall be whiter than snow," and "Rock of Ages, cleft for me," as he did when things were going well, and Richard did not have to pay much attention to the sermon because there was a picture of a woman and a baby on the front of his Sunday-school leaflet--Mary, the mother of Jesus--and he loved her face. There was a shadow of sorrow in her eyes, only she seemed to have gotten used to it so that it didn't interfere with her gladness over her baby, and in a way she reminded him of his mother, and he glanced sidewise to make sure. It was true, they were much the same, both so quiet and sweet and knowing they would be hurt. A rush of love for his mother welled up and filled his heart and trembled in his bones.

Walking home from church, his father spoke to his mother for the first time and said he would like cherry pie for dinner, and his mother was glad to make it, and they all strolled slowly through the edge of town down their own road, where the dusty goldenrod was hot in the sunlight and they could feel the burning of the pavement through their shoe soles, and his father took off his coat and carried it and rumbled snatches of the hymns in his bass voice, all the way to the door of the house.

It was the middle of the day, hot and torpid, a time that stretched and stayed, with sunlight blazing on the bare wooden walls inside the little workshop behind the house, and nothing alive that wanted to move--except his father, who was busy with a plane, making thin strips and curls of shavings peel off the piece of board that would be the new ladder rung, his father and the flies, which liked the heat and droned in endless circles and occasional downsweeps in the glare above their heads. His father showed him, very man-to-man, that this was a good sound piece of wood, the grain running lengthwise and no knots to spoil its strength, and he drank the knowledge in, sensing that this was his father's

secret of power, that there were things to be learned
and known, useful things that would come in handy and
that you could tell someone else and show that you
were a man who knew how to do things right.

Richard held the ladder firm while his father
took the brace and bit and bored out the pegs that had
held the broken rung. There were two nail holes in the
side of the ladder, and his father frowned at them.

"Where did these come from" Did you do this?"

"No, sir," Richard told him, glad that for once he
wasn't guilty. "Mother tried to mend it."

"Oh," his father said, and he darkened for a moment.
Then he clapped his hand on Richard's knee and let out
a low laugh. "Well," he said, "she's only a woman. You
can't expect her to have good sense."

He was treating Richard exactly as if he were Gordon,
sharing his knowledge with him, teaching him, starting
to laugh with him; and this about his mother was a joke
that his father and Gordon often made between
themselves. Now his father was waiting for a response
from him, and the moment drew out a little too long,
and Richard knew a fleeting panic that he might fail
his father and lose this new closeness. Only it hurt
him to joke about his mother, because this jest always
made her head lift a little and her face grow still
and contained; so, whereas Gordon would have laughed
out loud, very jolly, now Richard managed only, and
just in time, to smile. But his father saw it and was
satisfied.

They put the new rung in the vise, and his father held
it in place while Richard brought the jaws tight,
twirling the stout metal bar. His father had placed a
thin strip of smooth wood on either side of the rung,
to prevent the jaws of the vise from biting into the
newly planed surface.

"There's always a right and a wrong way of doing

anything," his father said proudly, with finality. A sentence to be remembered, a piece of knowledge, a part of his father's sureness--with the man's heavy voice giving it the final authority. But there was something perverse in Richard, something inside his mind that lightly mocked him as he tried to memorize for all time, for a new security: *There's always a right and a wrong way...* Suppose, the lightly mocking voice queried, suppose there are more than two ways? What if there are millions and millions--trillions and trillions? Wouldn't you get all mixed up? Only that was never true of his father. His father's sureness was a power so strong that everything moved aside for it. How did you learn to be so sure? Did you learn like this, one thing at a time, remembering forever which of two ways was right and which was wrong? But how did you get to the end? How did you know which two ways to start with?

Gordon grasped these matters instinctively. Gordon was like his father. It was a deep-seated despair in Richard that he could not see his way into his father's world, that he kept wandering through the richness of the earth in uncertainty, never quite finding his bearings. How was he to learn? How was he to know how to be so sure and final in judgment, in the midst of the kaleidoscopic profusion of things, when the surety itself was an alien place and whenever he tried to reach it the mocking questions raised their heads and he had to ask them? Only, it would never do to ask his father. "Of all the fool questions!" his father would say. That was certain. Richard knew that much. He had always looked like a fool to his father. Only today was amazingly different, with his father taking him in and teaching him, and he tried again to learn: *There's always a right and a wrong way of doing things*. But the words didn't come home to him. It was like trying to memorize a piece in school that didn't make sense. You began to repeat the words, but after you had said them a few times they weren't words any more -- the meaning went out of them. He began to roll them on his tongue: *wrong way, rong way, rongway*--a soft gong sound that was pleasant, a lovely noise in his throat, but it didn't mean anything at all.

Sweat from the close heat of the little shop stood on Richard's forehead in tiny beads, and a drop of it gathered and ran damply down his nose. It was splendid to be here with his father like this but it lasted so long. He wished they would stop work and go swimming. He and his mother always went in the river at this hot time of the day, before they ate, but his father would think the suggestion outrageous, with work to be done, so he kept quiet and just thought about it.

It would be wonderful to be hanging on to the edge of the big float anchored well out from the shore, and to dip down under the water where the shadow of the float made an expanse of deep green beneath the surface. The float was much too wide to swim across under; he was afraid he couldn't hold his breath that long, although he often tantalized himself by thinking of doing it; but it was exciting just to duck himself under the edge where the water was dark-bright, and to feel the heavy wood between himself and the sky.

This was the first summer he had learned to do more than dog-paddle in the water, although his crawl was still too quick and choppy and he couldn't keep it up for very long. Every day it was wonderful, with his mother, to leave the sun-drenched lawn, to hurry down the stairs between the slithering willows that grew in tall clumps beside the riverbank, to take off their shoes on the pebbles, and then to feel the sweet cold shock of the water as they waded in. The water was milky-green and a little brackish with the long upwash of tidewater from the ocean fifteen miles away. And after they had waded out arm-pit deep, feeling their way slowly over the slippery, rounded stones, if they stood still for a minute, the pale green fishes would come up to them and nibble at their legs.

He remembered how it had frightened him the first time it happened--the strong rubbery nibble on his thigh. He had screamed to his mother for help, and clung to her hand when she had swum to him. He was not an unusually timid boy, but he had been young, only seven, and the attack had been unexpected. Richard smiled now to think of what a cowardly custard he had been. But he remembered very clearly what had come next: how they had put their faces under water and how, after the first blur, they had stared through the distorted glassy water-world; feeling even now the enclosing touch of cool water around his head and reliving the watery vision of the fishes, not too far away, suspended, hardly moving--the flat, silver-green sides and the blunt snouts, the transparent quivering fins, and the single unwinking eye observing them without emotion--the round, the glassy, the unlidded eye.

"They were investigating us," his mother told him when they stood with their heads in the sunlight again, "to see whether we were good to eat."

"They're mean. They bit me," the boy insisted.

"No, that's not true," his mother said. "Meanness has nothing to do with it. They did bite you, but it wasn't much of a bite, when you come to think of it. We are something new in the water, and they had to find out what we are. They might have eaten us if they could, but our bodies are too big and alive and solid for them."

"What do they eat?"

"Oh, small fishes, water worms. They'll snap at very

odd things, bright bits of metal in the water, and they'll eat dead things."

"Would they eat us if we were dead?"

"Yes, I imagine they would. Dead bodies grow soft underwater; they're no use anymore. The fishes help to clean things up. The only thing for you to remember--" his mother's face grew intent as it did when she spoke seriously to him "--is that they don't do it from meanness, biting at anything, dead or alive. It's just the way they are. And it's very important to learn how things are. Not the way you're afraid they are, or wish they were. Not either one. How they *are*. You have to discover that the world isn't thinking about you, not lurking, lying in wait to harm you, although lots of people when they're young think that and are afraid it's so. And it isn't waiting, trying to please you, either. There are lot of things in the world that will bite you."

"Ants," he cried, from immediate experience.

"And bees, and snakes and spiders and fishes--lots of things. But the thing you have to learn," she said, very earnest, "is that they don't do it from choice, not from wishing to hurt. It's from a singleness of direction, a sort of simplicity of nature in them. There they are. They go their way, and sometimes it collides with your way, and they may hurt you. But not from meanness, not from desire. It's only people who are able to hurt from choice." Her face grew quiet from thinking. "And when people reach a singleness of direction, it seems to be a singleness that either wants to hurt or wants never to hurt--one or the other. The time will come when you have to choose. . . But that's too much for you," she cried, suddenly seeing him, so young. "The thing you have to remember is to meet things as they are, not to lie to yourself about them, not to fool yourself--not ever."

She suddenly smiled at him, very merry, and then, since he was too small to swim so far, she told him to hang on to the inflated inner-tube that he used to buoy himself over deep water, and she towed him out to the float, a vast heavy raft that swung up- or down-river against its moorings with the tide, a soggy wooden island, gray with long weathering and green with salt rust around the bolts; and they crawled up on its coarse, splintery surface, the old wood so water-logged that it floated half awash as they lay on it, watching the stretching water and soaking up the sun. . . .

"Hold the gluepot," his father ordered him, and he came back abruptly to the sweltering shop, to the drone of flies and the scent of wood shavings. "Take it up in a cloth. Don't burn your hands. That's right. Now see if you can hold it steady and not slop any of it."

Richard wrapped the pot in a thick rag and held it close to his father, concentrating on steadiness; and his nostrils were full of the acrid, nauseating odor of hot glue, as his father dipped a thin stick into the brown mass. He held the pot very hard and very upright, and even when the glue adhered to the stick and tried to pull against him, he did not let it tilt.

Dinner was on the porch again because of the heat, and it was late because Mother had stopped to bake the pie, and consequently his father was displeased with her. There was roast beef, brown and crusty on the outside but ruddy and oozing juice in the middle when the knife sliced into it, and there was lots of gravy for the mashed potatoes; and pretty soon, eating began to ease his father's annoyance, as it always did; and the first thing they knew, his father began to talk, to talk about Richard--to boast about him.

"The little son of a gun did all right," he said. "He's not such a fool as he looks when he runs wild. He held that gluepot steady as a rock, and it was heavy, and hot."

It was intoxicating, it was too heady--the sudden elevation to an approbation he had never tasted before. Richard began to puff up inside. He wanted to swagger. He wanted to shout. And all the time, his father's eyes were on his face with that keen glint of approval.

"Damned if he isn't going to be a chip off the old block," his father said, laughing, pleased at what he saw in him. "Give him time. He's a comer, this kid of mine."

Richard could hardly hold himself in. He felt terribly strong and fine. He wanted to gloat, the way his father did. There was something in him that his father liked, after all--liked and was proud of. He felt full of a fierce vigor, as if he could do anything, and burned with vainglory, the admiration in his father's face making leap and tug within him the prancing horses of his pride. Give him time; he'd learn to "lay it on the line," too. He'd show everybody.

When the cherry pie came on, his father tasted it judiciously. "A little too sweet for my taste," he said decidedly. "I like my cherry pie good and sharp, with a real tang to it. I don't think she quite hit it on this one. What do you say, son?" He turned to Richard, grinning at him, welcoming his opinion, welding the two of them together, the pride and force in the man laying hold upon the boy, raising him to a terrible stature, claiming him by the strong tie of their shared masculinity. The unfamiliar swollen headiness in the boy suddenly burst its bounds, and he broke out in laughter, drunk with power and position.

"Well," he said, "She's only a woman; you can't expect

her to have good sense."

His father guffawed with pleasure and reached around the table corner to slap him on the knee. And Richard looked up, straight into his mother's eyes, very wide and dark and startled, looking at him. Just for an instant her face was stricken and her mouth flinched, before she caught herself and her lips formed a small, strained smile. Then she made a gesture he'd seen in her before, when his father taunted her, she tossed her head up like a young animal, like a pony, the way she did when she came up out of the water, pulling off her cap and shaking her hair back to free her head from the underwater tightness. Then she smiled brightly at Richard, not forgiving him, not reproaching him--having recovered herself now--just liking him and seeing how it was with him.

But it was to Richard as if he had struck her. There she was, her face brave and bright--all alone now, betrayed in her love for him. If she had turned on him in anger, rising in honorable wrath to punish him, he would have welcomed it. He was all hollow inside, with his own horrid words ringing in his ears. And yet she only tossed her head in that high way of hers and smiled at him. He flung his napkin down and, mumbling "Please excuse me," bolted from the table.

"Hey," his father called after him, "don't you want your pie?"

"No thanks," he managed to get out. "I'm full." And he ran desperately down the steps from the porch and down across the lawn, his feet clumping monotonously, like weighted things, pounding out upon the grassy earth the leaden beat of his anguish.

He was sitting on a dark, twisted root at the riverbank, gazing outward, a slender web of trailing willow branches enshrouding him, spreading a transparent veil of green and silver leafage between him and the bright aching sky. And within him the gloomy, terrifying coils of darkness swirled--not creeping upon him from without, as his mind had always foreboded, but rising like brown and evil fumes from within himself, choking and sweeping down around his burdened heart. Oh, not from outside, whispering from corners, the brown horror threatened, but rising from within, the engulfing, sickly miasma of evil possibility, of evil done. The taste of revulsion at the easy power he had grasped and abused was brassy on his tongue, the thing he had done boiling like a cloud within him, cutting him off forever from sunlight and pleasant hours, from all future happiness. He ached to go back and live the last hour over again, to change it, wipe it out; but there it hung, implacable, achieved, not to be undone--the unendurable, the guilty, the irretrievable act lying between him and his life.

 He seemed to have been sitting there for hours, the sickness dark and heavy within him, the flush of shame curling in his flesh. And nothing changed, there was no escape, it would not go away. And he began to hate them, pulling him between them the way they did, his bitterness turning in its desperate unrelief into resentment, into blame--beginning now to want to hurt them, to injure, to punish them, and to flee then, far away--to escape, to stop feeling, to stop being anything--not to be anything at all. . .

 Then his father would be shocked and, for once in his life, ashamed, because it was really all his father's fault and his father would know it and would have to pay for it. The reason he had done what he had done, really, was to please his father. His father had intended him to do it. And his father would have to face what he had done, then; and he would groan, and even cry. And his mother would see, then, that he hadn't meant to; she would know how much he loved her because he hadn't been able to stand it. He stared over the water, his resolution growing stern and frightening within him; and there, far out, floated the moored raft, gray, sodden, half awash, and very wide, its wet surface twinkling under a thin pall of cloudy sunlight.

    He took off his shoes and socks on the pebbles, then let his Sunday trousers slip down around his ankles, and slid out of his shirt. He folded the discarded clothing carefully, ritualistically, and laid the neat little pile on the willow root.

    The river was cold after the hot air, and the ripples slid tingling over his body like reminders of all the summers he had known, as he dog-paddled outward, his muscles knotted and his breathing harsh and rapid. It surprised him that he reached the float so quickly, but everything was tight and dreamlike, and went too fast. He grasped the ancient, hairy wood with his hands, took three deep breaths as he did when he was going to surface-dive, and then pushed himself down and went under.

    The water under the raft was deep green and crystal clear, not fogged and thickened as it was where light lay on the surface. He swam a few strokes strongly through it, towards the darkness. Dark slippery weeds hung from the underside of the raft and tickled his back, and once his shoulders bumped against the old wood above him. He reached what must have been about the center of the raft and put a hand up, suspending himself for a moment in this strange underworld. His resolution was still strong and bitter within him, but the knives of anguish had ceased to cut into his heart with their keen edges; his heart held only a deep, recessive hurt, like a bruise. He tried to think about drowning, but his eyes kept seeing the water, bright as glass, and every moving shadow around him, and he couldn't think of anything.

A school of tiny minnows skittered past, turning and wheeling away from him, and then he saw the big ones, not swimming, just materializing out of their own element--the two large fishes, their flashing scales a pallid green in the underwater light, not moving, suspended but alive, seeing him there with their unblinking crystal-rimmed eyes. For the flick of an instant it occurred to him that they were hanging there waiting for his body to grow dead and soft and ready to be eaten, but the thought did not disturb him, and faded instantly. There they were, the beautiful shapes, so firm and shining and cold; and instantaneously all time fled away from him, and with it the silliness of anger and of being hurt and of shame. There they hung, almost close enough to touch--the bright fishes, with their little speckles and streaks and feathery fin lines and the clear bubble-like eyes from which their lives looked out at him; and swiftly, not with the deliberateness with which things move in time, but with the swiftness of thought, the waters swelled out and grew big, grew into all the waters he had ever known or dreamed of, all the waters since time began, all black resounding oceans tasting of brine that reached out long-threading fingers to him here in this brackish tidewash, and all sweet streaming rivers and great foaming falls, and small flat stagnant pools, green with scum and insect-haunted. And through them all forever, undisturbed, unchanged, vanishing and reappearing, moved the pale cold fishes, equable, unhurried, hungry, alive -- forever themselves and undecipherable -- forever from the first touch of life in the first waters.

The two cool metallic shapes that hung before him now

moved slightly, and he saw again how alive they were. And now, mysteriously, long streams of joy like cool green beams streamed out of them to him and out of him to them and lighted all the waters, and he was shaken with the wonder and the irreplaceable richness so that he could have cried out, and just as he knew he must shut his eyes to blot out for an instant the strain of beauty and unendurable bliss, the fishes suddenly flicked sideways, both as one, shimmered briefly against the darkness and were gone, leaving him wild and shaking, still suspended there in the liquid greenness, and all the terrible glory of the world and its vast waters was strong and sweet in his mouth. Then, because a vigorous and ennobling laughter filled him, he let out an expulsive blurt of breath and knew there was no air to draw in again, and he was halfway under the raft and his lungs were aching and his chest was pinched by an enormous hand.

    He moved then, motivated not by fear but only by a furious endurance, and began stroking toward the light. He would hold his breath one more stroke, and then one more, while the little bubbles oozed relentlessly out between his lips and his ribs caved and his head pounded and his throat was racked with strain, and he could not endure it, and made one stroke more, one stroke more. . . And there was air in his lungs, so harsh it seared them, and the weathered gray wood of the raft edge rasped against his cheek.

    He hung there while a long time passed, one arm clinging to the soggy old timbers, his straightened lungs still gasping and filling with the moist river air. He looked across the shining plate of the river to the silver willows, tranquil and undisturbed, and there on the beach he saw his mother in her faded red bathing suit, come down to join him. And even from out here he could see that her attitude, the set of her

Kressmann Taylor

body, was not as he had dreaded and pictured her, not touched by tragedy and awaiting expiation, not darkened and bent by grief; nor was there disappointment or schooled courage in her easy movement. She was just quietly there, in the hot smoky afternoon -- wading in now and reaching down to touch the cool of the river water with both hands.

#   #   #

Eleven Stories ... plus

THE MIDAS TREE (9)

 The oval mirror in its tarnished gold frame, over the cold drawing-room fireplace, glowed darkly in the late autumn light. Stella Tarrant opened the door from the dim hall and stood silently for a moment on the top of the three steps that led down into the room. Before she descended she moved to the exact center of the stair so that the mirror would catch her in its dusk-green shield with a slow and unfolding welcome as she came down. Her figure had a coltish grace as she tried to arrange herself, the shoulder bones still awkwardly youthful, the waist too tightly cinched in an attempt to achieve a slender elegance. Her mother, she had been told, had had a waist a man could span with his two hands. Stella put out one foot, intent, ceremonious. She descended softly, she felt, like a leaf floating, pointing her toes gingerly, seeing first the reflection of the long queenly feet, next the narrow waist, then the tilted, half-lifted arms that made so lovely, so tender a pattern, the white throat springing in a V from her dark dress; last the blurred white oval of the face with its great dark eyes. Standing on the carpeted floor, she held her post a moment, swaying slightly, absorbed with a sort of wonder in the distant, dream-like figure that, within the sea-green spaces of the glass, paused with her, swayed, waited.
 Outside the windows the heavy foliage of the ash tree was solid gold, the clean untarnished bulk of leafage in full daylight glowing like a great weight of metal--a Midas tree. Its brilliance so underlighted the green damask of the draperies looped across the narrow windows that the whole room was filled with a

green mist, a shifting, stirring water radiance. "Like a sea nymph in a salt sea pool," Stella murmured to her far-away image, herself entering now the strange water-brightness, water-darkness, crossing the room now, while within the mirror frame there moved also, grew larger, serenely and surely approached her, her cloudy-sweet, her oval face.

Because of the mirrors Stella was not alone in the harsh, too still house. All the dim decaying rooms hidden within the shell of ancient white cupolas and wooden gingerbread, the whole inside of the house, so hushed and laden with carpetings and fading brocaded fabrics, contained in every room at least one deep and unlighted mirror, as a forest contains its dark and unguessed pools, its secret springs. Into whatever room she moved, the face waited, her friend, the unknown one, the holder of secrets.

She paused now a few feet from the strange other-world of the glass, holding off the moment of completion, of coming quite face to face; and the strange undersea light of the afternoon troubled and delighted her, so that her heart began to beat heavily.

"Are you alive?" she murmured to the dark-eyed self before her, and the mirrored mouth moved and her own words went whispering through the room. Her heart beat rhythmically, like a floating gong, and the sea-green air hung still above her--a wave suspended. The onyx clock on the mantel ticked and ticked, but nothing moved.

A door closed upstairs, and she came back to herself. The room hardened to normality, to the threat of intrusion. She had almost neglected the last step of her ritual, and she moved hastily to confront the glass in a torment of despair and supplication, seeking the gaze of those unfathomable wide-spaced eyes, the pallid face tight-circled by its sheath of smooth dark hair. There was again that frightening moment of strangeness and of recognition. She caught her breath. It was a cryptic and wonderful thing to see her own dark mystery within the mirror, moving with her, sighing with her, yet apart, not even surely alive--a phantom, yet not unreal--unspeaking, this glass-enclosed figure, incapable of action not first created for her, but surely something, surely responsive, a presence--oh, unquestionably a presence, with eyes that gazed painfully and deeply into hers.

"Unseen, unseen. You are as yet unseen," she murmured to it, coming very close now while the swarming green air hung like a curtain of cloud around them both, and she could see sharply in the mirror the curling lashes, the tiny mole like a beauty spot on the chin, the plaintive mouthline cut so clean and tragic, its faint rose almost as colorless as the ivory cheeks. The eyes sought hers without choice, but asked the same dark question: Who are you? Who am I? What do we mean?

Ah, she loved her, this self, this dear one, this stranger. Her heart shook with joy and wonder. It is I, she thought, and so it was; but it was also someone else whom she could never reach, never touch--her darling, her friend, her soul, remote from her body, yet herself--her dear knowledge of her own dark beauty.

The noises from upstairs grew diverse, grew into tinkles and subdued thumps and rustlings, into droning voices and the movement of feet, came louder, came closer: Aunt Augusta's steps ponderous and implacable, Aunt Pris's click-clack of heels accompanied by the clatter of beads and bracelets, and finally, tardily, the slow masculine footsteps of her father, the weary undertone, the pivot of the unbearably stifled sad life of the house. In a moment they were around her in the drawing room.

"No hat, Stella?" Aunt Augusta, black and bosomy in her hard, high-necked taffeta, inquired in the set formula which implied that Stella was forever incapable of producing a suitable head covering. Aunt Augusta's face, wide, too large, and of a plate-like flatness, with its disfiguring lump of mole on the side of the nose, weighed upon the girl, imposed its stern heaviness of suspended judgment upon her, so that her uncertain secrets shrank and hid within the frail protection of her young flesh and she shivered from exposure whenever the chill unmoving eyes inspected her.

And above her father's fidgeting and irritable silence, Aunt Pris, rattling, rattling in her perpetual note of uneasy gaiety, about the young pastor: He had such a becoming pallor, but whether it came from spirituality or from anemia, who could tell? Her titillating giggle fluttered around the edges of, and coyly fingered, the ecclesiastical broadcloth.

"A slack mouth, perhaps, don't you think, Augusta? A little too full a lip for his chosen profession – couldn't you say?" And the nervous giggle -- oh, indecent, indecent -- while the glittering little eyes slithered around to Stella's face and nudged her with a coy eagerness that implied a community of understanding. The girl felt her face flush with shame and discomfort. What was it they thought of her, expected of her, these two women? She was uneasy with them; she could not make herself at home with them. Through all the long years of their guardianship of her, they had enclosed her in a fretting, zealous watchfulness that never failed to stir in her a feeling of uneasy guilt.

And her father's dim, troubled glance, he too

reproaching forever the thing she secretly was, the
girlhood in her, the floating softness of her life
which would not find its base where they all stood,
these adults, these fixed ones, bound and hardened by
the past events of their elderly lives, without hope
in them, without tomorrow; her father sensing how she
pulled away from him -- from them all, but from him most
fiercely, most imperiously. Ever since her breasts had
budded he had impinged upon her with this uneasy
restraint, this restless paternal rigor, lest something
rise and show itself in her that he most feared; yet at
the same time searching, probing, asking, the tight-
collared figure empty in its need, its fusty lack: the
man whose love forsook him in his youth -- her absent
mother, strange and greedy and denying them all. Her
father, uncomfortable with her, yet strongly encroaching
on her, forbidding her her identity -- saying nothing.

    She looked at him closely as he held the door for them
and they passed by him, the three women of his
household, remote, unloved. Her mother had left
him -- had left her, Stella, also, -- before she could
remember her; and her name was a wraith in the house,
a tight line on Aunt Augusta's lips, a scandalized
delight in Aunt Pris's agitated, unloved bosom -- for
her father, what? Did his dry fretfulness cover a
longing for the ardent, willful, impetuous girl who
was gone? (Her picture of her mother was inevitably a
romantic one.) Or was he secretly glad to be free of
that wildness, only his pride offended? She knew
nothing, actually. She knew only that his fretting
watchfulness of herself chafed her, irritated her,
drove her perforce into a secret, inexorable hiding
from them all, an exultant selfhood that locked itself
away and refused them.

    At the drawing-room door Aunt Pris suddenly wheeled

around. "A light," she murmured, hurrying back to a table and triumphantly turning on one bulb in a high, fringed lamp. "It's always better to leave a light burning."

"Nonsense, Pris." Aunt August was firm and commanding from the hall. "At this hour of the day! Don't be silly."

"An empty house," Aunt Pris affirmed, reappearing, leaving the light still burning, "invites intruders. It will be dusk before we get back. They say you should always leave a light on somewhere, or you just advertise that you're away. The best place of all is supposed to be the bathroom. I was reading only this week. A lighted bathroom--perhaps I ought to just slip upstairs before we leave."

"Pris." Aunt Augusta's bulk barred her way. "It's plain to see you don't have to pay the electric bills. Or even look at them. I'm the one who does the scrimping around here."

Aunt Pris bristled. "It's all very well, Augusta, to remind me of my position in this house. I was simply acting for our own good, our mutual good, for all of us. The times are badly unsettled; everyone knows that. Nobody can tell what moves the criminal mind nowadays. There was that man in New Jersey, a perfectly normal citizen as far as anyone could see, with a wife and children, even, I believe. And he suddenly seized a gun and started shooting everybody in sight. . ."

"Then," said Aunt Augusta, unmoved, "We'd be safer staying at home and not taking a walk."

"That was a mere case in point." Aunt Pris was quivering with irritation. Her sister's flat common sense always baffled her in argument. But with feminine illogic she would seize a former grievance and attack again. "And bringing up the electric bills," her voice went higher, "you know very well it's Harvey pays them, even if he does let you make out the cheques. Ask Harvey whether we can afford the risk of robbery, Augusta."

Stella saw that her father's fretfulness had mounted to exasperation barely held in check. The mention of money always disturbed him deeply as if he felt something indecent in discussing such matters. Although he wore his suits until nearly threadbare and although as the years went by and his position at the warehouse remained unimproved while prices inexorably mounted, the household had come to be maintained on lines of near parsimony, nevertheless he would never inquire the price of an article in a shop, but would make his selection from a showcase and then formally, painfully pay the sum asked, even when the price was beyond anything he had imagined. This was a matter of gentility with him, of family pride, even though the family had decayed past all saving and there was no more position to maintain. Now the argument of his sisters stirred this shame in him, and he suddenly whirled on the spare-hearted, bickering women in thin irascibility.

"Will you stop caterwauling?" Then, himself shocked by such a display of pique, turning away from them, red-wattled and indrawn: "Come on. Come along."

"Shall we leave the light?" Aunt August demanded.

"Leave it. Leave it," he cried, his wrinkled neck suffused with an irritable pink.

Aunt Augusta still got in the last word, albeit obliquely. She corrected his daughter.

"Your hat, Stella, Must we wait for you?"

Stella hastily pinned on her small black sailor before the too-bright hall mirror, apologetically, for she always reacted automatically to their commands--diffident, obedient to any of the three, timid, feeling her unsureness; only in her secret lovely hidden life daring to deny them, there alone essaying gleefully, desperately to follow her own sweet will.

The Sunday walk took them as always up the wide sidewalks of Chestnut Street, first past the tightly packed rows of square wooden boarding houses with broad front porches all alike, then through a more recently built development where the prettier brick and stucco residences, carefully dissimilar in plan, sat sedately among plots of lawn and low shrubbery--to the stone gates of the park. They walked slowly, the four of them abreast, her father on the outside with Aunt Augusta beside him, she herself between the two women, carefully shielded from passing contacts by an aunt on either hand. A drab but formal arrangement they made, this little human line, pausing when they met other pedestrians to allow the intruders to file by them, without breaking the stiff front of their narrow phalanx.

A young man passed them, strolling, and his eyes flicking across the four sedate faces were touched with amusement, then courteously lowered. Stella blushed and resented him. She saw themselves as he must see them, four carefully brushed and preserved figures from the days of carriages, shabby, respectable, proud, the women with their high-perched hats, her own face, already a young woman's, surmounted by a schoolgirlish round of felt. His face had reminded her of one of the boys at the painful monthly dancing classes of her early teens, where she had suffered, all clumsy big hands and feet, the impatient, forced partnership of innumerable boys with whom she stumbled awkwardly at arm's length in anguished apologeticness: "Oh, excuse me." "'Sall right." "I beg your pardon." "My fault." No conversation had ever proceeded beyond these brevities, and she had wondered enviously, passionately, how they did it, what they knew, those bright, squealing girls who whirled so fast.

The memory was a discomfort to her, and she was glad to reach the park gates and start down the flat path where the brisk autumn breeze rose to meet them, below the golden trees, toward the midnight blue of the little lake with its two rigid white blobs that were swans sailing lightly near the dock end, where people would sometimes throw bread to them. They were greedy things. On the hillside she saw that the cotoneaster berries were bright red, the naked black arms of the spraddled trees splotched with tiny pendants of red. "The year is bleeding itself to death in berries," she thought, for she often made such phrases to herself and sometimes wrote poems, which she hid away. The chrysanthemum beds were topped by masses of an odd reddish-brown flowering, like rust spots on the earth, as if the heavy old iron earth were rusting away, and she drew in her breath and sniffed their live musty odor on the sharp breeze of the dying day, of the dying year.

When they reached the lake she wished, as she had wished a number of times before, that she had got up enough courage to bring some bread for the swans, for nobody was feeding them and she liked to have them come near. She liked the coarse webbing of the wing feathers, the hard cold eye, the awkward, forceful angle of the feet, so ugly when they revealed themselves in their strong paddling. She came closest to forgetting herself and her strange, sad life when she was in the open like this and came near to the look and touch of natural objects, crude and unfinished things, hard, spongy, cold, resisting—tree bark, mushrooms, stones, and cold still water. Something satisfied her in the angular articulation of animal joints, the rude potency in them and the absence of prettiness. She wanted to touch and handle firm, resisting things, things that she had to face and brush flesh with without resort to dream or yearning. There was a sort of catharsis in these contacts, but after them she was always briefly frightened, as if nothing else real could ever be offered her in all her long-stretching life.

 She squatted suddenly by the lake shore and picked up a handful of gravel, rubbing it between her palms, not harshly so as to hurt, but just firmly enough to know its strong granular substance. She had so far forgotten the others standing there that she did not at first hear Aunt Augusta's startled reproof:

 "Stella! What on earth. . .?"

 Slowly she brushed away the bits of stone that clung to her hands, and then rinsed her palms in the shallow water. She rose to her feet in time to catch the knowing, despairing glance between her aunts, to savor fully her father's silent distaste for her act. Without another word they walked on, all four together, in a prim taciturnity that closed over and covered her shame. Her palms were wet and uncomfortable, but she dared not wipe them. She glanced at her father and noted with a sinking heart that he was in a frenzy of exasperation. His face was working, and the purpling cheeks were covered with a fine dew of perspiration. His long, ineffectual hands made little jerking movements in front of him and his protuberant Adam's apple moved up and down.

 "I can *not* understand it. I can *not* understand it!" he burst out harshly, and the look he turned on his daughter was one of furious reproach and distress, of cruel dislike and repudiation. *He hates me*, Stella thought, shrinking. *He cannot stand to have me alive.* Her heart turned hard. Why couldn't he leave her alone, then, she cried to herself. Why must he pull and tug and reach for her? He wanted her to be sorry for him, now; he wanted her to be ashamed of what she had done, for his sake. But inwardly she was not ashamed. She could not understand why that was such a terrible thing to have done. There wasn't anything wrong about it really, was there? Only, that was just her trouble. She never seemed to know. She was not instinctively decorous. The world these others inhabited was directed by values that were not familiar to her, yet it was a real world. She sensed its strong solidarity of substance and was frightened by it. She rejected it; she did not want it; but even if she had so willed, even if she had labored to belong, she would not have known how to become a part of it. There must be something wrong with her. There was always this dread and hope in her, this floating unrest, the sense of the impending wonderful, the secret barely withheld. Other people's lives, the ones she had known in school, her family, were too close and crowded, too full of bickering, too noisy. Yet everything fitted together comfortably for them, their acts, their days, their knowledge; and she was sick with envy of their ease in living, but she could not join them. She would never, never be able to belong anywhere.

  The four of them walked slowly, in severe formation, among the wild blazing of the autumn foliage. Aunt Pris was the first to forgive her. She broke the silence, making small gushing noises toward the golden loveliness of the park.

  "Ex*quis*ite, ex*quis*ite," she cried, with a jangle of bracelets in the direction of a grove of yellow birches.

    Stella gave her a stiff, brief smile of thanks, for although she felt ashamed of her aunt's silly exuberance, really she was grateful.

    The birches *were* lovely. They were like slender young girls with streaming hair. They were like young girls standing all alone, observed only by fantastic old women, loved only by fantastic old women with shrill, ungentle voices. Their gold was mirrored with wavering outline in the shore water of the lake, now blackening with the waning of day. The water seemed to deepen as it grew darker, and she remembered that someone had told her this lake had no bottom, and she fancied its shadowy night stretching down and down into the steely black heart of the earth. Through such a gateway, perhaps, Persephone, daughter of the warm earth goddess, had gone down long ago to her dark lover, through some such water that pierced the earth in far-away Greece or the white temples, Persephone, who every year was thus ravished once again. This flare of autumn color was the last sight earth would have of her until spring. The old tale seemed very real here between the midnight blue of the lake and the golden trees.

    This was the one thing she had kept and treasured from her school days at Miss Boynton's Academy, the town's select school for girls, where the family had somehow managed to send her as a day pupil and where she had spent four silent and unfriendly years, slipping in and out of classes unnoticed--her acquaintance with Greece and Rome, the wine-dark seas, the sunlight and tragic passions. For two timid years she had been half in love with Mr. Dawes, the professor of classics, who had a dramatic voice and would sometimes read aloud the old stories of white-armed Helen for whom the black ships sailed, of girlish Iphigeneia, slaughtered on the altar in her bridal garments, of golden Aphrodite, and of dark Dido, burning Dido who died in fire as the far sails grew small on the sea's horizon.

 Gradually she had come to dream of those ancient queens and goddesses, those lost and desperately beloved women, partly because Mr. Dawes' heart seemed devoted to them and thus she sometimes imagined that an hour would come when he would look up in class to see her sitting there and his eyes would come awake with recognition and he would say to himself, "Why, she is like them," Partly she identified herself with them because her fate was of their deeply yearning and unhappy kind. Their lives filled her with a delicious melancholy, a sweet desolation. They were her tragic sisters. Her own lost mother had been one of their tribe, her mother who had loved someone too well, who had been ravished by love and stolen away, to disappear, like Persephone, into a darkness that had never yielded her up again.

 Slowly and sedately the four figures strolled around the dark water, while the storm of autumn leafage raged and exulted around them in unashamed gaudiness and fury and abandon, and Stella's heart grew full of a quaking peace.

 They had late tea, as they did regularly one Sunday in every month, at Cousin Edda's on the far side of the park, a prosperous house with blocky large upholstery and boldly flowered draperies. Aside from the meetings of the Ladies' Aid and the Missionary Society of the Congregational Church, which her aunts attended regularly, this was the family's sole social contact. Cousin Albert, bald and paunchy and well dressed, lighted the gas log in the Georgian fireplace (they did not burn wood because Cousin Albert was assistant manager of the gas company). Stella did not like this house, partly because it made the Victorian clutter of her own home appear so shabby by contrast: it was so obviously affluent, although not dignified by beauty; and partly she disliked it because whenever she came here, Cousin Edda's daughter Doris made her uncomfortable.

    Doris was eighteen, two years older than Stella, very blonde and plump and assured of manner, with a soft, inviting mouth and knowing eyes which seemed to find Stella amusing. They were sly eyes that contained too much knowledge for her years, and they could see straight into Stella, exposing mercilessly her inmost secrets. They saw all the bitter poverty of her life, all the things that Stella lacked, and with acid perception saw, too, how much she wanted them. While their elders went through a cheerful recounting of minor illnesses in both families during the past month, the two girls sat opposite each other, carrying on a cruel, undisclosed warfare of the eyes -- the smiling, contemptuous attack, the naked, shaken, bitterly proud defense.

    Today, however, when Cousin Edda had carried away the teacups, Doris abruptly changed her manner. She took Stella upstairs to her own pink-ruffled bedroom and became cozy and confidential and girlish. Stella could hardly believe it. Here where she had least thought of finding friendship, it was being offered her. Her face flushed and she wished she had something to talk about that would be interesting, but she couldn't think of anything. She felt clumsy and uncouth, as she always did around Doris, but she kept smiling and listening, because everything was so pleasant. She felt now that she had imagined all those things about the way Doris looked at her. The bright head leaned closer, and the soft mouth whispered:

"Look, Stella, you have to tell me. Have you ever been 'kissed'?"

The word was curiously underlined, but Stella, in panic at the idea of disclosing the full depths of her loneliness, her un-sought-after state, was not fully conscious of it. She played for a frantic moment with a disclosure of the truth, then lowered her eyes, lied, and said yes.

She was not prepared for the extent of her cousin's astonishment--her blank disbelief.

"You, Stella! Honestly? You're not lying to me? Gosh, honestly I wouldn't have believed it of you. But how do you manage it? With those two old crows flapping around you all the time!" The loose, silly mouth became more knowing, more confidential, began to whisper shocking things, using terms that Stella had not known existed, whose meanings, for all her reading, she could only tremblingly suspect. Her whole body flushed with shame and distaste, but also, alas, with a furtive curiosity that drank in all she was hearing and that she hated in herself. Then Doris spoke her mother's name.

"They've all been so afraid you'd turn out like her, and here you are. . ."

It was only then that there entered Stella's consciousness the full realization of what she had been drawn into. In quick shame she shied away from the knowledge of her own participation; she flung her repulsion against Doris in the shape of anger, a burning, righteous defense of the beloved, tarnished woman who had borne her. Her mother, victim of sweet tragic love, to be touched by this prurient finger!

"You leave me mother alone. She wasn't like that."

And then Doris's shrewd eyes were taking her

all in again, probing her deceit, her ignorance, even her shameful interest, until she blushed scarlet.

"Well, you won't tell," Doris said. "You'd be afraid to."

When they reached home, Stella lingered in the drawing room, clinging to the protective presence of her aunts, even listening with satisfaction to Aunt Pris's long recital of congratulations on the un-robbed state of the house, her pleased vindication of the burning light bulb. It was good to be here, safe among the rubbed plush and fringes.

The next morning was dim and blurred with rain, and outside the windows yesterday's flaunting leaves hung drenched and sodden. All day she sought the company of her aunts, avoiding the mirrors, avoiding her own eyes, which had always been unabashed and clear, before, but which she now hesitated to meet. She was fretted and disturbed. For the first time in her life she had caught a taste of corruption, and her vision of the world as it might be was shaken. It was shaken because there was something in the evil, the ugliness, that she already knew. It was the recognition of this understanding in herself that frightened her.

Then, gradually, as the day drew near sunset, the skies began to clear, and though the ash tree was now sad and browning, there was enough gold left alive in it to reflect the pale rays of the declining sun. The beautiful bright dying of the day consoled her, restored her. When the last light began to fade out of the sky, she went to her room and shut the door and sat for a long time in the dusk. She was possessed by a tender melancholy. After an hour, or it might have been two or three (she had no sense of time), the night outside began to glow and quiver with light. Through the window she watched the great pale globe of the moon swim above the rooftops, laying its bold pallid light in swaths through the leaded panes, across the floor. She raised her eyes to the long mirror of her dressing table, and there outlined by moonlight, a faint and shimmering oval, her face regarded her with clear recognition, in all its remembered untarnished loveliness. This was the real world; here was the truth, the beauty, the hope of life to be entered. Doris could not touch her; none of them could touch her, here where she lived alone.

She was not sure why it was, but it was so. The hours of this interminable day had lengthened out into long separate periods, and all, as she remembered them, had had the ugly smell of decay about them. Not only because the year was dying in wetness and leaves going sour in the gutters. People's lives carry a bad odor, she decided, perhaps because of the things they concern themselves with. It was as if people kept looking for scabs and itches on their bodies, and new ones kept occurring. But her loneliness was a clean thing.

"Who am I, then," she murmured to the night, "who dwell in a white place, securely, bathed in starlight?" The question was poetry, but it was true. The night was akin to her. She belonged in these stillnesses.

She rose and stood, as was her wont, before the mirror. She thought again of Persephone and of Dido, tragically loved, and each of them wore her sad and wondering face. Whenever she thought of these lovely ones out of the past, she never once pictured the men who had loved them; she saw only the lonely women surrounded by adoration as by a brooding mist. She began to get ready for bed, still standing before the glass, observing in its darkness the grace of her movements as she stood in the moonlight pulling a petticoat over her head, twisting a slender shoulder and arm and tossing back her hair.

In a few minutes she stood unclothed, her young body white and shivering a little in the moonlight. The shoulder line was bony and thin, the cupped breasts stood apart, each tipped by its soft rosy bud, the navel a shadow on the flat belly, the knees pressed together, the white thighs rounding above them in the shape of a heart, its apex the little triangle of hair. Those others, too, had had beautiful bodies; they had been sweetly desired, pressed in love... Her heart began to beat slowly, deeply, like a tolling bell, and her body was shaken by it. She began to tremble; a terrible yearning suffused her for nothing she could name, and rose in her throat like choking. Every inch of her skin was intensely sensitive to the press of air; all her body was cool and alive.

"Oh, what -- what?" she whispered to the mirrored beauty, barely breathing. The air of the room was cold. Under its chill the soft tips of her breasts hardened and grew tight, as if the moon had touched her with fingers. She ran to her bed, hardly breathing and pulled the strong chilliness of the sheet over her, to her chin. Her eyelids shut out the moonlight.

The next day she only went through the motions of dressing, eating, speaking when she was spoken to. She was wrapped in a sense of revelation, of something promised, coming near. She still felt the moon's touch like a spell upon her, and the hours floated by like mist.

At the luncheon table her father (he always walked the ten blocks from the warehouse to have lunch at home) corrected her brusquely for day-dreaming. She turned her attention to the family scene far enough to encounter his face, the eyes moistly suspicious, the lean cheeks slightly weather-mottled, the whole a pressing, fretful intrusion upon her mood.

"I was only thinking of something," she told him impatiently. She would have none of him. She would have nothing of what they all planned for her, wanted for her, plotted to make her. She closed her mind to him as she would close a door.

After the meal her aunts departed with her father. They were to attend a meeting of the church missionary society. They counseled her as usual to keep the doors locked and to shake down the furnace at three o'clock, and she agreed patiently, her anxiety almost a palpable thing standing behind them to push them out.

Left alone, her spirit shook like a green bough. The buds of spring growth swelled with intolerable yearning against the hard confines of their woody shells. The green sea of the house washed over her its riches of ribbon-weedy waters and deep-ocean light. The kitchen tidied, she went strolling around the house almost mesmerized, idling upstairs and down. At the small deep-framed mirror in the turn of the stairs, she stopped and gazed for a long moment into her own glowing eyes, then laid her cheek against the glass and was startled by the coolness of the contact. Her face was burning.

When the doorbell rang, she was disquieted; she did not want to be intruded upon. For a moment she decided not to answer it, but curiosity sent her down the stairs. There were few callers who came to their door.

A young man, startlingly sharp with masculine presence, stood there with a package of cards in his hands and a big square envelope tucked under his arm. He had a frank cheerful face and curly, self-assured light hair and a stubby nose, and his eyes looked

straight at Stella as if he and she shared a rather
good-natured joke between them. He started talking the
instant she opened the door.

"Good afternoon, Miss. Miss Tarrant, isn't it?
I have a gift here for you. It's something I'm sure
you're going to like and appreciate. And it comes to
you absolutely free. You're not going to have to pay
me a single cent to get this beautiful gift."

"A gift?" Stella could not quite take in the startling
physical immediacy of the young man; his brightness
was of the quality of the autumn display of the ash
tree, an unexpected splendor that came unasked. And
the offer of a gift was so much in keeping with her
state of dreaming delight that the petals of her
spirit did not shrink together as on another day they
might have done. The arrival of such a messenger
bearing gifts seemed touched by the same poetry as the
promise of the night. The appearance of the young man
at her door was both improbable and startlingly real.
He stood there smiling, superb, expectant. His
swiftness and confidence simply coiled around her like
the movement of a wave, so that she was surrounded by
it, caught in it, feeling her feet shift unescapably
under her.

"But how do you know who I am?" she asked. "Who's
sending me the gift? I don't understand." Yet the heat
in her veins whispered to her that whatever this was,
it was to be expected. She had asked a gift of life,
and it was in the literal terms of a gift that she was
being answered.

"Now before you say a word," he said eagerly, and his
voice was pleasant and full of a sunny forcefulness,
"I tell you what I want to do. I want to show you this
beautiful gift." He transferred all the cards to one
hand and took out the envelope, which he fumbled to
open with the hand that held the cards. He was so

good-natured about it, laughing at his own awkwardness and finally handing the cards to Stella to hold for him, that before she quite knew how it happened and forgetful of the repeated family warnings about letting strangers into the house, she found the young man was inside, was an incredible presence in the hall, and she was showing him into the drawing room, where he sat down on the horsehair sofa with her and spread out the cards on the low table, on Aunt Augusta's lace doily, where they had no business being and looked so strange they altered the whole room, intruded quite brazenly upon its shadowy, cloistered life; and in the transformed room the presence of the young man was resonant as a trumpet.

He was well knit, vibrant in his bodily movements, and he handled the cards and envelopes easily, after his preliminary clumsiness at the door. He took the beautiful gift out of the envelope and looked at it, cocking his head sidewise; and it was a large colored picture of Niagara Falls.

But this was absurd! Stella felt a little dizzy and was perturbed because her expectations were going awry. He laid the print on the sofa between them and began to explain in a lively voice how important it was for every family to have the right number of magazines and how you could get out of touch with the world by neglecting to keep up with the right kind of reading matter, and how there were special magazines for every kind of reader, young or old.

So he was a magazine salesman. After her first shock and abashment, which left her feeling foolish that she had expected so much (hoping the gift would be something rare, liking the messenger), Stella was still not so much let down as she might have been, because his presence was so overwhelmingly strong. Her swift shy hope should have been quenched entirely, but instead she found herself caught up by his pleasing manner, still anticipating something more, as she sat and watched him. In itself it was astonishing to have the young man sitting there, so substantial and masculine and full of cheer, with his hands moving among the cards and his voice reading off the names of magazines he wanted to recommend to her. She began to wonder at the clever manner in which he seemed to defer to her opinion but still didn't let her interrupt, to wonder increasingly that this could be really happening, the young man with the short nose and the curls almost like an Apollo's so unexpectedly filling the room with himself and his talk.

    The picture of Niagara Falls, it appeared, was a gift you got absolutely free by taking three subscriptions, and Stella thought it resembled the cover of the calendar their butcher gave out at New Year's, the one they hung on the back of the kitchen door. Anyway, she knew they would never in the world take three subscriptions, but she didn't tell him so because she wanted him to go on talking. Several times when he mentioned a magazine whose name she was familiar with, she let her face look interested and receptive, and then he would begin to describe that magazine explicitly, being very hearty, so that her heart misgave her for the deception she was practicing, though she rejected its prod.

    The young man was going to college and was selling magazines on his free afternoons to help pay his way, he told her. And here he stopped, as if he were thinking to himself, and then said that it wasn't really college, it was art school, but he was supposed to say he was going to college.

    The admission, the careful correction, made a sharp appeal to Stella's honesty and shamed her, for he was being fair where she was not, and she was lowered by it in her own eyes and troubled. Perhaps, as in the old tales, there were rules to the mythical happenings of this day, and perhaps by her false encouragement she had broken a rule; or perhaps she was only properly following what curious rules there were. She had begun by offering a cheat for a cheat, for the bright chromo which was not a gift at all, her bright attention which promised an interest she did not have in his wares. Some further expectation had come alive in her; a spring of solitary hope had been touched by the young man with the fair hair, the jaunty bright face, and she did not feel the constraint that usually took her in the company of young people, but felt as if he were already an old and somehow cherished acquaintance. Still, her feigned interest put her in a false position, and she shied away from acknowledging her first credulity and her present shamming. She floundered in herself, and then the preposterous nature of what he had just said, about being an art student, and his having praised the gaudy picture struck her, and she knew a harsh need to show him she was a person in her own right, to put him in the wrong.

"You go to art school?" she asked him boldly.

"Yes," the young man said, and for the first time he looked at her somewhat truculently. "Yes, I honestly go to art school. What about it?"

The encounter seemed to be dictating its own terms; she was obliged to meet him and not be overwhelmed either by his presence or by the idiocy of what was going on. Stella tipped her chin indignantly away from the chromo of Niagara Falls. "But you told me that was beautiful, and it isn't. It's hideous." How dare she be so monstrous and so forward!

Her boldness was successful. The young man leaned back in the sofa and rocked with laughter. He was so amused, he thought it such an enormous joke that Stella, suddenly secure, had to smile with him. She felt the stirring in herself of a power she had never before experienced--a little heady, exciting.

"Miss Tarrant," he said, "you're priceless. How did I ever happen to come on you?" Although he was not asking this question of her but of himself, the swift, unexpected pleasure of it lifted in Stella's heart like the flirt of a bird wing.

"How do you know my name?" she asked, still feeling daring, wanting to establish his awareness of her, his response to her boldness. It had been very startling to be called by her name. His knowing her name had been the introduction to this whole strange encounter and was the thing that had at once seemed to make him known to her.

He turned his eyes to her and gave her face a lightly considering appraisal that suddenly made her uneasy, although his gaze was not unfriendly.

"Check," he said finally. "All right if you want to know, I asked the people next door 'Who lives there?' and they told me Tarrants. Simple when you know how. Standard sales technique." His voice was amused and faintly ironic.

"But you pretended you knew me," Stella protested. Swiftly she was hurt and badly let down; the warm flush of blood in her veins was checked and baffled. She wished desperately that there had been more to it than this. She saw that she had been taken advantage of in a way that, after all, was hardly fair, that was chilling. " I don't think that was honest," she said.

The young man laughed incredulously, but this time he was frankly laughing at her. "Now why" he mocked, eyeing her askant, "do you expect me to be honest? Do you think people are going to open the door to a salesman and ask him to come in? Of course they aren't. Not in this rough world! Nobody wants to see me and nobody wants to listen to me. But I got in here easily enough, didn't I?"

"You cheated me," Stella said obstinately, wishing it didn't seem so pleasant to have the young man here, with his firm lively body squared away on the sofa and his eyes aware of her -- not when he made her feel just like anyone else, any customer. And he *had* taken advantage of her! "Anyway," she said firmly, resolving to clear the decks of her own false cargo of lies and of hope, "*I'll* be honest. I'm not going to buy any of your magazines."

"Check again," the young man said, and now he grinned at her in a way that was quite audacious and made her catch her breath. "Tell me, how would you know I'd fooled you to get in here if I hadn't been honest enough to own up?" He laughed. "It's always my charmingly frank and open nature that does me out of a sale, and now I've done it again. You aren't going to buy any magazines because I was honest enough to tell you the truth. That's irony for you, isn't it?" He looked quizzically at her.

"In a way, you're right," Stella said painstakingly, feeling that in some part of his talk he was still deceptive, twisting things, exerting a false pressure on her. She saw that her own lying was not wholly cleared away and she was at a terrible disadvantage before his self-mockery until she might be free of it. "The reason I am not going to buy any magazines," she said stoutly and sullenly, looking at her lap, "is because I don't have any money at all. And my aunts would never dream of buying any. They would throw a mammoth fit" she said, lapsing into schoolgirl slang, "if they knew I'd even talked to you."

"Well," he said in a refreshed voice, "so now we have all the cards on the table. And who's been fooling who? So you knew you couldn't take any, but still you let me go through my whole spiel." He was teasing her, and it was somehow good-natured teasing, yet he was frightening; he had seen too much, and if he had glimpsed all her softness and her eagerness toward him. . . Don't let him really guess the way I thought it was at first, she demanded in inner fright.

"It wasn't like that," she insisted, sharply on the defensive. "You wouldn't let me talk. You're still trying to make things look different from the way they were." Her voice was sulky. "Anyway, what's a spiel?" she asked, to get away from a subject that made her miserably uncomfortable.

"Honestly," he said, and this time his eyes were bright and full of a different kind of liking for her, "I find you hard to believe in, and I trust this isn't an act. Don't you know anything? Didn't you ever hear of a selling spiel? Did you think I was making up that whole line I was handing you, as I went along? We memorize that stuff, honey," he said, becoming too quickly familiar. "We take a course in sales technique, and we're drilled in every word. It's just a patter. We have to take tests in it."

Stella was startled and withdrew a little at the familiarity. His hands put the cards together and his look was turned too closely upon her, speculative, with something lying behind the look that no man had ever shown her before yet that was over-familiar, was in a coarse and obtrusive way like Doris's knowledge. She wanted to dislike the way he looked at her, but not to reject him entirely, not to end all this or cut it away -- not to have nothing happen to her ever again while the long days closed in on her in her accustomed solitude.

"I would hate it," she told him, keeping her voice distant, "having to convince people and not meaning what I said."

"Look," he said, squaring around to face her but still maintaining his easy ascendancy; "it's a rough world, Miss Tarrant, and everybody's trying to get his out of it. Personally, I'm going to get a lot out of it before I'm through, and so I use my assets. I've got a good personality." He smiled at her knowingly, wickedly. "Don't you think I've got a good personality?"

Such impertinence must not be taken personally. Stella blushed, tried to gather her forces and put off the encroachment of his look. She forced herself to attend to his question and to deliberate about his personality. It was true. He had force and an easy-going charm that she felt strongly.

"Yes, you have," she pronounced soberly.

He laughed again. He did laugh a lot. "So why not use it? That's the way it is in this world. I can make people enjoy listening to me, and I get a kick out of it. Suppose I do kid them? Everybody's making a fool out of somebody else, I figure. And I do pretty well at it. Most people like to be fooled. Buy a package of dream stuff--life with the movie stars for three seventy-five a year; so I give them what they want. Sure I lie to them. My rule is, tell the truth when you have to, but lie like hell to cover it up."

He seemed to be deliberately baiting her, and this time he had succeeded. Stella was shocked, and now that her own conscience was cleared and her disappointment hidden, she was able to feel virtuously indignant. "But don't you mean anything you say?"

He found her protest amusing. "Most of it's patter, but of course you have to have a feeling for different types of people, figure out how to carry them along. You've got to have a natural talent for it." Again his personal appraisal was close to insult. She could see that he was actually pleased with the traits he was describing in himself, for the look he gave her was relaxed and lenient.

"Do you mean you figure out how to manage people like me?" This question hurt, was a thorn in the flesh of her pride, but her desire to know obliged her to ask it.

"Sure. All kinds. Now don't take offense. Usually we're not encouraged to get inside the door with young girls; you can see how that might not always be so good. But you're all right, the intelligent type. Just say I find it flattering to see how far I can get you to go along."

"Is that about the intelligent type part of your plan?" Stella was again disturbed by her inner uncertainty. Why was it that while she disliked and distrusted everything the young man was telling her about herself, she should find herself drawn by the simple fact of his being here, and even being attracted by the knowing frankness with which he revealed his depravity?

Her question did not disconcert him. "Sure," he said. "It's all sales talk. Or not entirely. You didn't like that Niagara Falls pitch for one minute, did you? I got that. You were leading me on there, keeping quiet to see how far I'd go with it, weren't you? And if I hadn't seen through you, the shoe would have been on the other foot. What price honesty now?"

"You're twisting everything," Stella said furiously, really caught out now and abashed by the toil she had woven for herself.

"You just don't want to admit it," he admonished her, poking fun at her; but there was a twinkle in his eye and she didn't know whom he was laughing at. "The trouble is, you want your motives to appear virtuous. Don't you know that nobody likes virtue? Oh, I know everybody pretends to admire it; everybody even pretends to have it; but it would be nasty if you really had to. So why try to make yourself look good to yourself?"

As she listened, evaluating his words, startled, receiving a meaning that was new to her, a slow light illuminated Stella's mind. This was the truth about herself: her own virtue had been a pretense, and she had defended it the more angrily to hide from herself the stain of her inner perfidy -- herself hiding from herself. She was shaken. However far she might probe into her inner mind, would she ever be able to encounter her central self, her final self?

"Now I am reasonably honest," the young man said. He laughed again. "I know all my faults and cultivate them. And I'll tell you, the only thing that matters is to see straight."

"I think so too," Stella insisted, in the frankness of the new honesty she was learning. "I really think so too. I admire that in you, only. . ."

"Only you'd rather I'd lie and pretend to have noble thoughts." His look was mocking and slyly personal.

She was checked. This was unfamiliar ground, and again he came too close. "Is there anything wrong with noble thoughts?"

"All right, honey, you go ahead and have them, or pretend to have them. If you want to be that serious." HIs words shrugged her off, but his eyes dared her with their look of challenge and male freedom.

"I do think one ought to be serious," Stella said, baffled by the paradox in him, but now wanting intensely, only, to get through to him, to make him see--feeling a little desperate, thinking that if only he would let her, she could somehow emerge as his equal and meet him on grounds where he would not scorn her. "I think life should be serious, and very wonderful--" her face grew lovely in its sober intentness--"and very real," she faltered, fumbling and feeling her words to be pretentious and inadequate. "You know what I mean -- with everything there is, all the time? It ought to be wonderful. It shouldn't shut us in always, the way it does. I think everywhere you go, well, there ought to be doors that would open to you. . ." She came to a halt, feeling very intense and full of pain. He was looking at her with a look of interest that encroached upon her physically, that was queerly comprehending and intimate.

"So what did you think, beautiful," he asked in a voice grown lazy, "when the door opened and you found me there?"

"You didn't let me have time to think," she said. He had called her beautiful. Her guard was down, her heart fluttering because of the personal question, his recognition of her, the new tone in his voice. "I did think you were nice" she admitted, flushing. "Otherwise, I wouldn't have let you in."

"You liked me?"

Now something more was happening. Now the personal attraction in his voice was all for her, and his sure masculine power allied itself with her own candor and forced her to respond.

"Yes, I guess I did." Stella kept her eyes down. Watching her there, braced valiantly at the end of the sofa, he could see her coltish shyness warmed by feminine self-consciousness, a posed grace in the posture of the slim arms, the curve of the neck.

"And what about it now, now that you so thoroughly disapprove of me? Do you still like me?" His voice was almost insolent, but his eyes were brightly confident, challenging and compelling. They exerted power over her.

Stella's face was hot. She was beyond her depth, feeling the frightening fleshly strength of him and, against all her knowledge, wanting something to happen. She said, "Yes, I do."

He let out a peal of low laughter, half ironic and half very gratified. "All right, sweetheart, I'm glad you like me," he said. He thought a moment and then looked at her with impudent familiarity. "And when you let me go on talking, instead of saying primly, 'No subscriptions, thank you,' and showing me the door--yes, you were even egging me on, weren't you?--what was the reason for that?"

Stella gulped, flushing again, her shame laid wholly open to the light. She was overcome by his penetration and his dominance, but was filled with a growing consciousness that he enjoyed her confusion and the knowledge of her falseness, that he was using her confusion to unite them in a curiously heated mutual nearness. She looked down at her hands. "I wanted you to stay," she said in very low voice, and the admission was a letting down of the gates, a surrender of some close-kept wholeness in herself.

He gave a low laugh, but this time just gratified. "Well, what do you think of that?" he said lightly, talking to himself. He put out his hand and took hold of her hand. "Now then," he said, and his voice was familiar and flippant, "I suppose I should leave and get back to work." But he did not move. His eyes, pleased and warmly oppressive, intrusive, were powerfully aware of her. "Suppose you give your Uncle Don a kiss. Hmm?" His hand over hers was big and close. His physical sureness warned her of something, but she did not wish to be warned.

"Oh, no," she said instinctively. But something in her wanted to, terribly. Something in her floated to the surface and acclaimed itself in all the haughtiness and delight and self-knowledge of abandonment, and she began to respond with a crazy kind of exultancy and guilt. His hand slid up her arm, and she said, "No," again, but her heart leaped painfully, and she let her eyes lift for one brief instant to his and say yes. Then his arms were around her and his mouth was moving over her mouth.

His touch was not what she had expected; it was not kind. There was something coarse and rough in the way he took hold of her, and she was startled by the aggressiveness of his big hands on her, by the unfamiliarity of him and his crude physical presumption. Again his mouth came down on hers, quite savagely, and at once everything was wildly wrong. His big male body reeked of animal heat. And his mouth -- this was nothing in the world like what she had imagined a kiss would be like -- not a tender touching of the lips, but his mouth was loose-lipped and slobbery and his tongue was moving against her teeth. He was breathing hard. All her virginal clarity shivered and caught on fire with fear. She shrank and put up her hands to push him away, and he caught her wrists in one hand contemptuously and twisted them aside and forced her against him. One of his hands ripped open the buttons of her blouse and clutched her breast in bold violation of her private flesh, and she began frantically, blindly to fight him, jerking her hands away, beating with her fists at his chest, at his red and panting face. In her mind a scream of fright began and went on and on, and she fought and writhed away from him, cold to the bone and wholly terrified, while his hands kept hold of her, kept possession of her in crude and familiar and intrusive exploration. She beat at his arms.

All at once, he let her go. He glared at her, his face loose and full of something ugly, but furiously angry, and he said, "All right, sister, if that's the way you want it. Only next time don't ask for it if you aren't ready for it."

The early afternoon sunlight, streaming full and metallic and undisturbed, embraced the young man's raging figure in a hard shaft of brassy light but left Stella shrinking in shadow in shocked fury. Now they both stood up, stood apart, staring at each other in violent antagonism and hatred.

Stella shuddered and pulled the dangling halves of her blouse together and stood quivering, near exhaustion, braced for flight.

"Please get out," she whispered with tight, bloodless lips. "Go away. Now."

He stood regarding her harshly, pulling himself together, not moving, and finally he gave a short laugh. "How old are you?" he asked.

She said, "Sixteen," as if she were compelled to answer, and he made a wry face and said, "My mistake," in his former tone of irony. He bent to pick up the cards and tried to smooth out the picture of Niagara Falls, which had become bent and crinkled during their struggle.

"Want this?" he asked, holding it out to her as if he were sneering at both of them, and she couldn't talk but could only shake her head, and he said crudely "Thought you might like a souvenir."

At the door of the room he turned around and looked at her, and his face was hard and mocking. "I don't go to art school, either," he said. The door of the room closed behind him, and in a moment or two she heard the outside door slam.

# #

Kressmann Taylor

FIRST LOVE (10)

(aka THE GREY BIRD)

  The garden was so full of bloom, so lavish of scent in this haze of light before the mists broke and let the sun through that Anna could hardly bear it. The grass was weighted with dewdrops through which she walked barefooted, her feet soaking wet, to the perennial border, where the white peonies exploded like great popcorn balls, poppies flamed the color of fire, and iris quivered in bunches of velvet blue. Nothing could be so regal, so overpowering; it seemed unbelievable to Anna that the flowers should reach such swollen heights of beauty all at once. She could not bear to have the sun show through, drink up the dewdrops, bring the hot day, imperceptibly dry and tarnish this cold perfection of petal masses.
  Everything is made perfect, she thought; this morning only, everything is in perfection. A shadow skimmed across her mind, and a gray bird, a shy rain cuckoo drifted like a shadow across the garden, spreading tail and wings broad to brake his flight. For an instant, before his feet touched and grasped, the underfeathering of the wings flashed white, and then he landed, the wings folded, and he stood tilting on the back of a garden chair, a gray bird in a gray light.
  Nothing white and perfect will stay, she thought, and was touched by a wild and terrible sorrow. And this premonition was new to her in her youth, this awareness of tarnish and change. "Let me keep it," she said aloud, insistently, wanting to stop time from moving on at all, looking with intense eyes at the massed plumage of the peonies, white and silvered with waterdrops. A voice said in her mind: This is the day of my disenchantment, the day that will bring my final sorrow with it before the last

shadows, I am sure of it. She blinked away tears, and there the flowers stood, white and hot gold and blue. It cannot change, it cannot change, she thought, I can't bear it.

Her mother called her from the house: "Anna," and her solitude was shattered. Her mother's voice was never impatient, always serenely sure of itself, always in control. "Anna dear," with a lilt of affection and reproof, "is that quite wise?" She meant, of course, Anna's being in the garden in her bare feet and Anna's never really thinking enough about her health, that great gift which young people took too much for granted, and of course she was right, at the same time that she was horribly, unreachably wrong. Anna ducked her head in apology and came trailing back across the grass and into the morning room, where the family was at breakfast. At each plate stood a slender glass of tomato juice, and Anna saw that her mother had used the tulip-red mats and the blue pottery dishes she thought so charming, and they would have to drink tomato juice because orange juice would have spoiled the color scheme.

Anna was amused that she knew these things about her mother, was able to see how charmingly her mother manipulated their existence, arranged a surface pattern full of generosity and prettiness; but underneath there was always the tomato juice, the sacrifice of the orange juice, which they all liked better, for the sake of the feminine and arbitrary order she placed before them. Like a gift, Anna thought.

Mrs. Jaines began at once, in her winning and persuasive way, to make plans for a buffet supper in the garden that evening. She had provided something special for each one, something to put a shine on the coming party: for Anna, the young McCrearys to play tennis before they all ate; for little Paul and Frederick, hot dogs they might grill themselves; and for her husband to enjoy, an old school friend of his wife's, Fran Adams, Fran Carruthers now. (The Carrutherses' arrival in town was Mrs. Jaines' reason for making a party of it.) Fran had been a very handsome girl, and Mr. Jaines would surely enjoy looking at her, if her looks had held up over the years. Mrs. Jaines preened herself, imperceptibly to everyone save Anna, the least fluting of a butterfly wing; for Mrs. Jaines, with her flawless skin, certainly had held up, so that people were always crying out: "It can't be possible you have a seventeen-year-old daughter?" However, Mr. Jaines believed it was all for him, the party, the planning. It was unthinkable to Anna that he should be so blind, that he did not see how deftly he was being handled. But he saw nothing.

Anna was furious. She showed it by saying irritably, "how on earth are we to have tennis with only Rob and Olive?" Her mother gave her a quick intelligent glance, which saw straight through to the source of her irritability and acknowledged the whole scheme of womanly duplicity without a trace of shame. But what she said was, "Oh, I should have mentioned. There's a Carruthers boy. He'll certainly be able to give you a game of tennis." Then rising, she said pleasantly to Anna, who was still fuming, "Help me clear, darling and then come upstairs with me. I picked up a smidgin of something for you yesterday."

The "smidgin of something" when the flat box lay open, turned out to be a tennis frock, very straight and simple the way Anna liked, and of the palest, palest yellow to suit her shoulder-length dark hair. Anna gave a gasp and buried her head in her mother's shoulder. "Mommy, I'm a beast."

"Why don't you try it on, dear?" Mrs. Jaines asked without a trace of smugness. "Only don't wrinkle it. I thought perhaps you'd like to wear it this

Eleven Stories ... plus

afternoon." There was not a hint of ulterior motive about her.

"I love it," Anna said. "I just love it." She kissed her mother and, holding the box before her like a tray of jewels, went marching down the hall, humming in her satisfaction and her surrender.

For her mother was perceptive about her, saw immediately what suited her. Anna thought: I don't deserve a mother like her. She is really too indulgent of me, and as a result I am becoming carping and spoiled. Her mother's voice floated to her down the hall: "Don't forget to put your shoes on before you come down."

And straightway that spoiled it, took the high edge off her gratitude. If only Mother would let me be myself for ten minutes! For that was the trouble, really. Her mother *arranged* too much. She simply did not allow things to happen, but was always putting them into a pleasant, suitable order. I wonder if she ever sees through to the wide dark places underneath, the terror and fright and the unendurable endings of things. She doesn't ever see how the whiteness of the peonies hurts because it is going to perish. Something is all wrong with the world. Look at the things that endure, like gravestones; it is the beautiful things that go away quickly, mornings like this one and iris blooms with their furred and spotted caves inside the petals.

At four in the afternoon, when Anna, after showering leisurely, came running prettily downstairs in her yellow tennis dress, the Carruthers boy had wandered away and was not in the garden, and she met only the parents, who were something of a letdown. Anna wandered away to the tennis court, where Rob McCreary and his sister Olive were batting balls at each other across the net, but not playing.

Rob came over to Anna at once, while Olive sent a ball sizzling past him in a rage, because he always forgot his sister immediately when Anna appeared, and even now his cheerful, good-looking face was going soft and humble with gentle, child-like devotion. Anna gave him a brief smile.

"Go ahead and play," she said to him, for Olive's sake. "I'll just watch until our lost guest gets back from wherever he's gone to." Rob obeyed her, although it was plain he didn't want to. I really shouldn't be so brutal to him, she thought, watching how dejected he was and simply flopping around the court. Only there are times I wholly can't stand him, and especially on such a blue day, such a clean, flag-waving day, with all the flowers out.

Rob and Olive hadn't finished the first set, when Mrs. Jaines called them to come meet the Carruthers boy. By the peony bed Anna saw a thin and sandy-haired boy not much taller than herself, with an expressionless and waiting face. He looked quite a bit older, possibly twenty, and held himself in a rather disdainful way. While Mrs. Jaines introduced Olive and Rob, the young man looked at Anna, and his face was too bold.

"This is Derek," her mother said, "And this is Anna," drawing her forward in much the manner of a mother hen lifting one wing half archly, half defensively to let the world observe her chick. Only under the mother wing, said this glance. My precious child, said the tone of voice.

"I shall call her Ann," the young man said in a cold voice. His look had settled upon Anna's eyes, and the boldness and effrontery of his regard were overwhelming. His brown eyes saw straight into the depths of her with a glance so probing, so pitiless and at the same time so personal that she was stricken and could only think: Why, he knows me. He knows me somehow immediately, secretly, in my hidden life. His cold look was cruelly intimate. I am alone, it said. I do not allow anyone to come near me in my aloofness. I am tragic and alone. Yet I know you; I knew you at once. We are alike and together, the young who live on the dark side of the moon. His solitariness and his daring set them apart from the chattering and oblivious group that ringed them round, and left them together in a sacred and honest and brutal place. And her shaking heart said, trembling with discovery: So this is what life means, this first knowledge of another. And in one glance of timid recognition, before she dropped her eyes, she gave him her whole heart out of her body, and stood defenseless in a flood of joy that was also fright.

Olive said petulantly. "We've been waiting forever for you to get back for the tennis."

And the strange boy said harshly, "Tennis? I don't mind, if there's anybody who can play. I hate taking on duffers." Oh, he was insolent, he was arrogant, he was wholly and forever set apart in his furious proud selfhood from all the common ruck of humanity. Derek, she thought, his name is Derek. A name full of beauty and fierceness.

They were all four sauntering toward the tennis court. "Where were you?" Olive asked. "Why did you disappear?"

"Oh," he said, very offhand, "I found a pond down there" and Anna knew a moment of complete bliss, for the pond with its trailing willows, in the midst of briars and wild land, was her own place to seek utter solitude.

"You must have liked it a lot to spend so long mooning around there," said Rob in his flat way, which would never comprehend anything.

"Why shouldn't he like it?" Anna asked angrily.

"You like it"? Derek asked in a hard tone and looked at her with eyes that held no invitation to her at all.

Anna gathered all her honesty and courage and said firmly, "You know perfectly well I would like it," And then there was the look again, and at the end of it in Derek's eyes she saw a little smoky blur of satisfaction.

To allow one good player on each side, Derek and Anna played partners, and this too seemed to be a sign fateful. At first she was afraid of his scorn for poor players, and once when she netted the ball he said, "What a muff!" But he had a marvelous eye and took most of the difficult shots, moving over the court in a furious sort of dancing. His clipped voice made demands on her and would shout, "Net, net!" or "Way back, Ann." She obeyed and let him use her and consequently she played better than usual and they took two straight sets, and then Derek was bored and didn't want to go on.

Going back to the garden Anna said, feeling that something was demanded of her, "You play beautifully," and Derek said languidly, "Anything I decide to do, I do well. Only I don't find many things worth doing." He moved up to walk with Anna and spoke directly to her one finger flicking the yellow frock: "You dress well." She blushed, warm with pleasure, but Derek had gone off onto some other tack.

The day had grown hotter and the air thick, and thunderheads were piled ominously high in the west. Mrs. Jaines told them to go in and shower before time for food, but Derek joined the men around the outdoor fireplace and was given a highball. He was going to eat in his tennis things.

Anna decided to wear the yellow dress for supper ("You dress well"); besides it would make them both dressed alike. But at supper Derek stayed with the men and seemed to have forgotten her, and she was nice to Rob and tried not to look over at Derek's back, so impervious and withdrawn.

By now the thunderheads had distended and blackened half the sky, and a wild wind rose that blew the paper napkins all over the garden, and everybody began to pick things up and hurry indoors. Just as they reached the shelter of the porch, there was a whoosh and the rain came down in silver plates and crashed on the roof with a din that drowned their voices. Anna loved it. She stood by the rail and shivered at the violence of it. A line of fire streaked through the black with a spitting sound which cracked and bloomed into thunder, so near it shook the house. Somebody said, "That's too close," and they all moved indoors.

Anna shook her damp hair, and her exultancy carried her over to Derek beside the fire. "Isn't it wonderful?" she asked. Now standing loose and haughty in the firelight, damp and disheveled by wind and rain, he looked so wild and beautiful that her heart melted and she let all her love shine in her eyes, inviting him to receive her and her joy. Only the miracle had grown thin, for while his eyes saw into her as before, this time they saw her eagerness, her thrusting toward him and a little veil slid over his pupils and he smiled, but to himself, not to her. "Yes, it's nice" he said dryly and looked bored and lifeless.

A sheet of rain swept coldly across Anna's mind. But against the chill her love flared and fought with a desperate clamor, and she began to talk very brightly, making her mouth gay, while her mind throbbed.

"I always go out in thunderstorms," she chattered. "My family think it's simply crazy of me, but then I'm always doing crazy things that nobody else does. That's just the way I am." The words were all wrong, hollow and childish, the sort of thing that simply mustn't be said. For she was trying to draw him back, to put the look into talk, and everything she longed for just suddenly sagged and died.

In despair she turned toward the fire and archly tilted her head and shook her dark hair in the warmth so that the fire would shine on it and bring out the highlights. He said smugly, just under his breath, "I don't like long hair." The words were an arrow; feathered and shafted by him and aimed deliberately straight at her breast. She blanched with the impact, and her heart drained white and her eyes were immediately hot with tears. He was cruel, he was cruel. She hated him. A line of poetry laid its whips upon her:

I fall upon the thorns of life! I bleed! He had willfully destroyed her, and she loved him.

Mrs. Jaines, coming through the doorway with the coffee urn, said sharply, "Anna you're cold. You look positively ill. Go and change at once."

In her room, Anna was stony and without tears. She could not yet understand what had happened, why he had not wanted what he had so powerfully asked for. He had lifted her up, flown her aloft to his wild height, and then had negligently let her drop among the barren rocks, and her loss was as bitter as death.

He was cruel. But she had been aware of that from the beginning. Part of it was her fault for melting so, and she blushed with shame. Even so, he had asked. He had demanded. And now there was only the wound of the beak in her side, the whir of hawk wings fleeting away. She would love him forever. She would carry this sorrow with her all her life, and no one would ever know She remembered her premonition of the morning: all glory is a brief thing.

When she came silently into the living room again, the Carrutherses were leaving, and Derek was thumbing the piano keys, self-absorbed. Everybody got up to go, except for Rob. Derek said good-by to Anna's parents and then stopped by Anna and said passively, "Bye, Ann. Nice game." Anna wanted to cry out bitterly, "It was not. It was not a nice game. It wasn't fair!" but she made her mouth smile stiffly, although her eyes were sick and told him her sorrow. She said, "Bye." She watched him go out the door, insolently, easily, not looking back.

As soon as he was gone, she realized what she should have said. Lightly, with a touch of his own scorn, she should have said, "Was it? I thought it was a bit too one-sided." That would have pierced his boredom, and she would have had a flicker of amusement and respect from his eyes, before he left, before he left forever.

Her parents came back from seeing the cars off, and Mrs. Jaines observed that the Carrutherses were a little disappointing. And Rob added his complaint and said that that snide boy, Derek, had gone off by himself and spoiled the tennis. Mr. Jaines thought that boy was bad-mannered, a self-centered pup. Anna said Derek played better tennis than any of them.

"I think Anna has a crush on him," Frederick piped.

"You shut up!" Anna said furiously, and Mrs. Jaines looked at her with curiosity and penetration. It wasn't going to be easy, Anna realized, to hide her secret.

Anna sat on the railing. A mist from the rain

touched her face, the sky wept for her, steady cold tears, and she gazed out on the wreck of the garden. How much did she have to remember, to keep, out of all the sweetness and the anguish? He had spoken to her directly hardly at all. Except for the orders shouted in the game, he had said only four things to her; "I shall call her Ann," "You like it?" "You dress well" and, unendurable but intended, "I don't like long hair."

That was not all, of course. That was nothing. But the other could not be talked about. It could only be felt, felt and suffered. The touch of the eyes, the knowing, and the fact that he had wanted to hurt her, had liked hurting her. A temptation came to her to turn to Rob and be sweet to him and make him adore her.

But even the pain, even the savagery of the hurt, she would not give up. It was better than what she would go back to if she let Rob comfort her. The pain and the joy were strangely mingled. She would not refuse the agony, which was all that remained. She stared out through the falling rain. The peonies were shattered and a fringe of sodden petals littered the grass.

Always, after beauty, there came the unendurable ending of things. She had learned, on her dark flight, that life, below the surface, is an unbearable robbery, through which she would always be reaching her hands to clasp the thing that would never last in her fingers.

Only the love lasts, she thought painfully. And she turned her head away from Rob, intending to let a tear come out, but found instead that she did not want to cry. Leave weeping and self-pity to children, who had not seen life with both its faces. For she knew that although she might come, in time, to agree with her father that Derek was bad-mannered and a self-centered pup (as she half-sensed already), not

Eleven Stories ... plus

again would she pretend to herself, nor ever lie to herself for comfort, since she had learned the loss and denial that are the dark side of the moon.

A car entered the driveway. The Carrutherses had forgotten something and come back. Anna said, "Excuse me," to Rob and slipped off the railing and went indoors and up to her room. Not to hide. There was just no reason to see him again. She wanted neither satisfaction against him nor renewal of promise from him. Voices sounded downstairs and feet clicking. A chair scraped, and then voices, Derek's among them, on the porch. She was unmoved. She waited silently in the rainy light, in a sort of fulfillment, a stern inner blooming, until she heard the car go down the drive.

#   #   #

Kressmann Taylor

MICHAEL (11)

When a boy gives his heart to a dog, he'll do anything
to keep him, even if the dog doesn't belong to him...

"Now, Michael, we want you to be very happy here," Mrs. Munsey said in a shrill, clear voice, as she and Mr. Munsey brought Mike, straight from the train, into the big bright living room where the clean, sunburned people were sitting around drinking out of glasses and all talking at the same time. When Michael and the Munseys came in, the talking stopped as if it were a radio that someone had shut off, and everybody looked at them.

"For these two weeks," Mrs. Munsey said, "you're to be just like our own boy, just like Joel." Joel, who had been with them at the station and had so far only said "Hi!" to Michael, lagged behind his parents and the visiting slum child, out of sight and out of reach.

"We expect you," Mrs. Munsey went on brightly, "we want you to respect our things, to keep yourself reasonably clean, and to answer politely. Otherwise, you're free to enjoy yourself." Mrs. Munsey smiled, and Mike, hopeful but strongly on the defensive because the people and the place were so strange and bewildering, understood that she was speaking mainly for the benefit of the other people in the room.

"You'll be given the same allowance that Joel has," the bright voice went on, "fifty cents a week, and I hope you won't spend it all the first day." She laughed knowingly, and one of the women in the room gave a little gurgling sound of approval and amusement. Mike sensed that they were laughing at him. Instantaneously he hated Mrs. Munsey, and he wanted to make a face at her; only he didn't dare to.

Mrs. Munsey led Michael around the circle, introducing

him, and the people looked at him brightly, interestedly, as if he were some sort of animal on show. Only, at the end of the circle, one large gray-haired man stood up when Michael was introduced, shook the boy's hand seriously in a large strong hand, and said, "How do you do, sir?" looking down at Mike out of grave eyes that seemed to see him as a person and like him. A first touch of genuine friendliness in this desert of faces that looked all derisive, it sent a crack opening along the hard childish wall of Mike's defensiveness; he felt his lip quiver, and he turned sharply away lest his weakness be detected. And then Mrs. Munsey, fortunately, took over. Joel was directed to take Michael upstairs and show him his room and get him into a set of Joel's country clothes, and Mike followed his ten-year-old host out of the bright room, and up the waxy stairs.

    In the sunlit bedroom, the two boys stood and stared at each other. They were the same age, but Joel was larger, had more meat on his bones, was safely at home in all the opulence and cleanliness; the city boy was darker of hair, pale of skin, and his great receptive brown eyes were on guard; they showed a touch of sharpness, bitterly learned in the canny, crowded, handcart-cluttered streets.

    Although, before Michael's arrival, Joel had been tutored to show kindness to the underprivileged child, his instructions had been colored by his parents' own condescension, however well meaning; and observing now the self-protective glitter in Michael's eye, he without compunction took charge. Michael was small and mean-looking and Joel felt that the two weeks didn't look very promising.

    "Do you ride?" he demanded.

    This was a foreign language to Mike. "I rode here on

the train," he said.

Joel snorted. The slum boy was not going to be much fun if he was stupid. "Can you ride a horse?"

"No," said Mike, shrinking because he had made a mistake, but keeping his eyes hard. Who rode horses? In his world horses pulled carts, shabby, drooping horses.

"Do you swim?"

This obviously was Michael's second chance, and here also he had nothing to offer. He dared a lie. "I don't swim very good," he declared, modifying the falsehood.

"Oh, shucks," Joel said. "I ride and swim most of the time. What *can* you do?"

"I can fight," Mike said fiercely.

"You better not try any fighting here," Joel said in a lordly manner. "My mother won't stand for it. My mother said you might be tough. If you're too tough she might send you packing back where you came from."

He found that he hated Joel worse than he hated Mrs. Munsey. The larger boy stood looking at him in an inquisitive manner.

"Well, you'd better change," he said after some minutes. "Your bathroom's in there, and Mother says you have to take a shower before you put on my clothes."

This time Mike understood. "I got scrubbed last night," he said. "I ain't dirty." With a wave of homesickness, he saw his mother's dedicated, tired face, as she had put him into the kitchen sink and scoured him until his skin was red.

Joel looked startled and his eyes changed as if it were possible he saw the whole picture right in front of him. "While you're here," he said in an instructive tone, which to Mike sounded condescending, "you've got to bathe twice a day, once when you get up in the morning and once when you come in to get dressed for dinner." He pointed to the bed, where Mike saw pressed

Eleven Stories ... plus

new brown shorts and a striped shirt laid out.

Beyond the far door was a gleaming bathroom, in which everything was glass and silver. Alone and free to admire, Mike was overawed. He was scared of getting things mussed up, the place shone so, and after he had stepped out of the steaming shafts of water, he shined everything up with the big bath towel, glass walls, floor, and all, until the towel was sopping wet. Then he didn't know where to hang it. He put on the patched underwear he had worn from home, clean that morning. But the Bermudas were too long for him and he was embarrassed by the unfitting borrowed clothes.

On the way down to show Michael the barns, Joel was important. "We have one hundred and twenty-five registered Guernseys," he announced, "and three of them are top prize winners." Mike did not know what Guernseys were, but he did not ask. In the barns he learned. The huge, sleek, reddish-gold heavy flanked, swaying and stirring live beasts, with a sweetish smell steaming from their bodies, stood in long menacing ranks, shifting in their silvery metal stanchions, and moving their big horned heads. They were being milked, an unbelievable anatomical process accomplished through shining aluminum milking machines by two efficient men in white overalls. Joel walked familiarly along the ranks of dangerous horns, stopping to call a beast by name and with bold hand reach in to scratch and fondle the wide forehead. Mike, his spirit cowering, walked behind him, overcome by these masses of powerful life, feeling ignorant and out of it. He began to wish he might take this courageous Joel across a New York street among the screeching taxicabs, to see how brave he would be then.

Dinner in this strange house was very late, eight o'clock. Mike was so hungry he was hollow, but he was even hollower at the thought of meeting again the scornful people, and when he came reluctantly down the stairs, in unfamiliar coat and tie, behind Joel, he was enormously relieved to discover that everyone had gone except for the Munseys and the older man whom he had liked, who appeared to be called Uncle Joe. Mrs. Munsey said, "Michael, you must wring out your towel before you hang it up. What did you do, drop it in the shower?"

At the table, at the start of the main course, Mr. Munsey said decisively, with masculine suddenness, "Don't you supposed we can do *something* about table manners" This can't go on for two weeks!"

Uncle Joe said quickly, "Look here, fellow, suppose we don't pick up the chop in our fingers. See if you can't cut the meat off it. Like this," and he showed Mike how, on his own plate with knife and fork, but he looked apologetic, as if he and Mike really knew a more sensible way and all this was simply to please Mr. and Mrs. Munsey. But Mike was stricken and didn't know what to do with his greasy fingers, because he simply hadn't noticed how the others were eating, he was so starved, and he immediately wished an explosion would happen and carry off Mr. Munsey and Uncle Joe as well. After that he wasn't able to eat much, and he was still hungry when the good dinner was over.

Michael had never slept alone before. Lying in bed that night, with the pallid light throwing moon leaves across the walls, he was frightened by the stillness, which made the room like a vast dark cave. Once in a while a dog would howl, far off, and the trees outside the window made little hissing, shuffling noises, and he kept remembering how safe and comfortable it was at home, in the narrow bed with his little brother Pete, and how the room flashed with red neon light from the beer joint on the corner and how the trucks rattled

Eleven Stories ... plus

and raced their motors and sometimes would pop their exhaust, and people's radios were going, and boys yelling on the sidewalks and footsteps banging in the O'Briens' flat upstairs.

In the morning Joel took him outdoors and showed him the horse stables and the pool. On the big back lawn Michael was introduced to an aristocratic dog of great size, a pedigreed golden retriever named Duchess, and Duchess licked the hands of both the boys and then lay down with her head between her paws and ignored them. Mike was a little awed by her, but he liked her better than anything else that lived here.

Pretty soon Joel went off to ride, and Michael was left to knock about alone.

That afternoon he and Joel went in the swimming pool, and it immediately became apparent that Michael could not swim at all. He launched out boldly at the shallow end, threshing his arms furiously but his skinny body went straight down. Joel just looked at him and then went up to the deep end, where he swam rapidly in circles or climbed on the board and did dives. After a while he joined Mike in the shallow water and they had a fight, splashing water at each other.

While they dried and dressed, Joel said that the farm had six hundred and forty acres and his father was a banker and a gentleman farmer. "What does your father do?" he said, looking at Mike.

Michael, daunted, fighting against magnificence, hit upon the noblest profession of which he had cognizance. "He's a policeman," he said boldly.

"You're a liar; he is not," Joel came back at him "He's a janitor. It said so in the letter Mother got. He's a janitor and he has a crippled leg."

"He is not!" Mike shouted. "He's a policeman. He's a policeman."

171

Michael had a good deal of time to himself. Joel rode during the mornings, and when in the afternoons the crowds of people came in to drink and bask in the house or on the lawns, Mike stayed away from them, because some of them liked to call him over and ask him questions and they would laugh at his answers and talk about him while he was there. Uncle Joe had gone away. One day when Michael wouldn't answer a woman in a red dress, who had a mocking face, Mrs. Munsey told him almost sharply to run off and amuse himself. "I'm afraid he's not a responsive child," he heard her tell the woman in red.

Michael's strangeness, his unfamiliarity with the laws of this new world, was the thing that drew down a continual mild reproof upon his actions, that laid him open to pain and shame. Michael did not own a toothbrush! Inconceivable! He was supplied with one and instructed to use it. Michael did not clean his fingernails. He did not change his underwear! Michael went through the door ahead of Mrs. Munsey, without waiting for her to go first. "Poor lamb," Mrs. Munsey said complacently, "at least he'll have learned a little something about sanitation and good manners by the time he goes back."

The Munseys thought they were being very kind to Michael. There had been two evenings on which the boys were taken to the moving pictures, and afterward Joel and Michael each spent thirty-five cents of their fifty-cent allowances for a double chocolate malted milk at the soda fountain.

It was on an afternoon early in Michael's second week that the extraordinary event took place. Joel and Michael had been sent out through one of the meadows to take Duchess for a long run. They were getting better acquainted, and they had run and walked and thrown stones at a tree, while the golden dog streaked far ahead. She went out of sight in a shallow ravine, and they ran to catch up with her. When they sighted her she was standing, head proudly erect and arched tail flagging her pleasure, sniffing nose to nose with another dog. Joel shouted at her and went charging in to separate the animals.

Storming, he led his pet back, hand hooked in her collar. "That's extremely dangerous," he told Mike angrily. "That's how dogs get distemper, getting smelled by some old stray or other." He jerked at Duchess' collar as if his impatience could undo the damage. "I'll take her home. Don't you let that other dog follow."

The other dog was following, albeit at a distance. He was a good-sized dog with a rusty coat and thick white ruff, and he was trotting happily along in complete innocence of any harm-doing, halting now and then to snap at some insect his passage had roused among the grasses or in the air. When he saw Mike standing still in his path, he cocked his head and then came bouncing and prancing toward the boy and leaped up on him, the big forepaws on the small shoulders. He licked Mike all over his face and neck. Mike was both startled and delighted. He said, "Down boy," because the dog's vast lickings were really overpowering, and the dog jumped down, his whole rear end wagging, and proceeded to lick lavishly Mike's hands and arms. The dog's impulsiveness unbalanced Mike, who sat down abruptly in the grass; thereupon the dog flopped itself down across his lap, where it churned and wagged and made pleased barking noises. "All right, get off," Mike told it, and the dog finally sat up a foot away and regarded him with big, dark, friendly eyes, its pink tongue hanging out. It was a very handsome dog, Mike saw. It had a white muzzle, with a white streak going up over its head between rust-colored ears and it had a fine golden-rusty coat and a white stomach and white paws. The tip of its tail, when that plume waved out at the side, was white too. ("Mostly collie," Uncle Joe was to tell him later, "a good breed.") Mike, his eyes absorbing these points of excellence, felt content and full of wonder, and the dog sat there quivering and gazed affectionately at him.

"Come here." Mike said finally, and the dog lumbered over and started to lick Mike's hand again, but then stopped and looked up at the boy's face to see if it was all right to lick. He was waiting to see if Mike would let him. He wanted to do what Mike wanted him to do.

The idea grew in the boy's mind like a broadening light. The knowledge stood in his head as clearly printed as the divine handwriting upon an ancient wall: *This dog is mine.*

"Lie down," he said sternly, and after considerable pushing, the dog lay down with the boy's hands on its shoulders.

"Barney," Mike said (the name came to him just that suddenly). "Come here, Barney." And Barney came.

The chief difficulty, Mike discovered, was to keep Barney, trustful and attached so quickly, from following him back to the house. Even without Joel's warning, intuition told the child that the big lolloping dog no more than he belonged in the world of the Munseys. But commands to go back had no effect. Finally Mike, Indian fashion, crept upon the stables from the rear and managed to steal a short piece of frayed rope, which he tied around the dog's neck. He led Barney back through the meadow and secured him with the rope, within a sheltering clump of willows. Mrs. Stevens, who was the housekeeper, approached doubtfully and not fully confided in, consented to part with bread and meat scraps.

"Now don't go getting yourself into trouble," she said dubiously.

That evening, Mike, troubled by the sweet responsibilities of ownership, confided in Joel.

"Maybe he belongs to somebody," Joel pointed out. "Has he got a collar?"

"No."

"Then he's a mutt," Joel said contemptuously. "You don't want a dog like that."

"I do, too," Mike said belligerently.

"You've got to go home in four days. What are you going to do with him?"

"I'm gonta take him with me."

"How can you?" Joel was impatient. "If he hasn't got a collar or a license, they won't let him on the train. They'll take him away from you and kill him with chloroform. That's what they do with strays that don't have a license."

This new possibility was too dark to be borne. "I'll get him a collar and a license," Mike declared with bleak assurance.

"What with?" Joel was hard and realistic. "How much money have you got?"

"Twenty cents," Mike admitted. He sensed at once that this sum was inadequate. "How much do they cost?"

"A license," Joel said positively, "will probably cost about two dollars, and I don't know how much a collar is, but it'll be plenty. So what are you going to do?"

"Maybe your ma'll give me a job," suggested Mike, grasping at a straw.

"My mother's doing enough for you now," Joel said with finality, "without paying you for some old job she doesn't want done."

"I don't care," Mike said, "I'll get it."

But he cared so terribly that his soul was sick. He spent the next morning in the meadow, frolicking with the big animal, which, released from the rope, raced and tumbled frantically, trustful and without apprehension, sensing nothing of the doom that hung implacably over the heads of them both. There was nothing else for it: it was up to Mike to save him, to save both of them.

After lunch Mike approached. Mrs. Stevens, "How can I get a job? I've got to make some money."

"Well, I don't know," Mrs. Stevens said speculatively, her eyes brooding over Michael, who was too earnest, too intense for her liking. "Danielses, up the road, are picking cherries. Maybe they'd give you a job picking; maybe they wouldn't."

Mr. Daniels, a bland, blond countryman, was not encouraging. "You're too little to move ladders," he said.

"I can." Mike told him. "I'm strong."

It was finally arranged that Mike be allowed to pick off stepladders and off the lower limbs at ten cents an eight-quart bucket. At the end of the day, grimy and aching and tired enough to drop, Mike had filled three buckets. But the thirty cents, with the twenty he already had, made half a dollar. Three more days, and he would have enough for the license.

At the Munseys that afternoon, there was concern. Michael had simply disappeared; he was nowhere on the place. When he finally dragged in at seven, black with dirt and spray residue and gummy with cherry juice Mrs. Munsey let out all her anxiety and exasperation and relief.

"Michael, you mustn't do things like this! To go off without letting us know where you were and make us worry about you all day! I don't care what you want, you're not going back again. Not unless you want to have your vacation end the first minute we find you off the place."

It was impossible to explain. Explain, and have the men find Barney and knock him in the head? And there were three more days. There is no hopelessness so deep as a child's. Michael was too sick to eat his dinner.

Next morning a new catastrophe threatened. On his way to the meadow before he had passed the stable Mike was greeted by a yipping, rollicking avalanche of fur and pink tongue. Barney had chewed the rope through and was loose and had come hunting for him. "Here, boy," Mike whispered desperately. "Here, boy. Shut up! They're going to kill you." He was crying when he hid the dog in an empty box stall. He was cold-eyed and hard of mouth when he entered the house, determined that he was going to do something, something, if he had to die of it!

Perhaps the very intensity of the prayer of the hopeless creates the conditions for its own fulfillment. Maybe the divine eye is not relentlessly blind. But salvation is not given easily. Mike prowled the house for two hours, in growing anguish and desperation. And then just before the lunch hour, wandering toward the haven of the kitchen, he discovered on the wide shelf in the pantry a number of sheets of printed paper, and each one had money clipped to it: the top one had two five-dollar bills. He did not understand that Mrs. Munsey had thus taken care of the tradesmen's accounts. In the world Michael had inhabited, anybody who wanted to keep his money hung on to it. Loose money was for the taking, or how else were the sharp and penniless young to survive? Nevertheless, the trusting manner in which the money had been left checked Mike at once. You couldn't steal from somebody who counted so obviously on people being square. Only the vision of Barney bloody of coat and dying, his confidence in Mike betrayed, his happiness stilled, moved the boy harshly forward. He would borrow the money, he decided, and pay them back as soon as he could make some. Feeling sick, he slipped the top five-dollar bill from its clip and wadded it in his pocket. Then, as first payment in restitution, he took out two dimes, a quarter and a nickel, and laid them in its place. Like a shadow, guilty, desolate, ready for martyrdom, he slipped out of the house.

When he was brought back just at lunch time (Mr. Munsey in the car had picked him up by the roadside, still a mile from the town), he faced the family in the hall.

"I'm afraid it has to be a case for the police." Mrs. Munsey kept saying in her high voice (the five dollars had been found immediately). "After all we've tried to do for him! The boy is no better than a common thief."

"I don't know, Mildred," Mr. Munsey said uneasily. "The kid has to go back, of course, but couldn't we let the agency handle it? He's pretty young."

"Encourage juvenile delinquency?" Mrs. Munsey said.

"Suppose you let me ask," said a calm, pleasantly deep voice, and Mike through his fog of anguish was startled to see that Uncle Joe was there with them, "why he put the fifty cents back."

"What does it matter?" Mrs. Munsey asked indignantly. "Fifty cents! He took five dollars." She looked outraged.

"If you ask me, he took four dollars and a half." He spoke to Michael, "What did you want the money for fellow?"

Even this degree of kindness was too much. Mike's defense broke down, and he wailed and clutched at Uncle Joe. "Don't let them kill him!" he howled.

"Confound it," said Uncle Joe to Mr. Munsey in the latter's study. "What in the name of all that's merciful, can the youngster do with that dog in the city? His family can't afford to feed an extra appetite as big as that one. And the dog can't run."

"Why don't I tell him we'll keep the dog?" asked Mr. Munsey, who was feeling contrite. "Then when the boy's gone, we can have the brute put out of the way. The kid doesn't have to know."

"If I believe in anything at all," Uncle Joe said ruminatively, "I have to believe that there are some human requisites that take precedence over circumstances and even over the pressure of my own convenience. The trouble is that when a man reaches my age, his life is pretty well laid out for him, and there are a good many demands already established. It has to be a question how far you let some new obligation interfere with what you can comfortably handle. Or do you," he asked thoughtfully, knocking out the bowl of his pipe in a flat brass ash tray, "do you have a right, as a human being, to fall back on your own comfort when it's a question of a child's need?"

"I can't help feeling we've been remiss here," Mr. Munsey said.

"The boy needed love," Uncle Joe said soberly. "That takes more effort and willingness than most of us are prepared to offer. Plucky little duffer," he said. "I like him. I think there's good stuff in that boy. Think of the fifty cents," he said, and he smiled to himself. "By Jove, no!" he said emphatically, "It will cost me something in time and inconvenience, but sometimes I'm not sure that most of our charity's not just paying out money to escape making the real gift. I'll keep the dog," he said, "take him over to my place and bring the boy out weekends to see him and play with him. Maybe something could be done, later, about schools, too."

"That's taking on too much," Mr. Munsey said. "You'll regret it."

"Maybe I will," Uncle Joe said mildly. "Maybe I will." He looked out the window of the study to where Michael and the lumbering rust-colored dog were playing on the lawn. "And maybe I won't," he said.

# # #

Kressmann Taylor

NOTES ON SIX OF THE STORIES

Of the eleven stories in this collection, I know of the background for some, but not all:

"Take a Carriage, Madam" was written at the request of my father in 1935, when he was editor of *Controversy*, a quite radical magazine for its day. The magazine had a fiction contest but got very few entries. Finally he asked Kathrine if she would write a story and enter it. She did so anonymously, under the pseudonym "Sarah B. Kennedy," and won the contest, which was judged independently of my father. This I know only from her report, as that was the year I was born.

"The Blown Rose" was first published in *Woman's Day,* (September, 1953) and later dramatized on *Westinghouse Studio One*, as "They Served the Muses," 1954(?). It was a story inspired by an old couple whom my parents knew in San Francisco when they were first married.

"Goat Song," 1955, and "Girl in a Blue Rayon Dress," 1958, were inspired by memories of country people living near the farm in Kerby, Oregon in the 1930s.

"The Pale Green Fishes," 1953, was first published in *Woman's Day* (May,1953), and later chosen for inclusion in *Best American Short Stories of 1954*. It is a story loosely based on my own relationship with my parents, and was not popular with my older siblings. I, however, considered it both honest and perceptive.

"The Red Slayer," 1955, published in *Woman's Day* (February,1956), was inspired by an incident on the farm at Gettysburg, involving my younger brother Jonathan and a bothersome woodchuck who had taken up residence beneath our house. My young brother shot the animal from an upstairs window, only to learn that it was a mother with very young offspring. My mother reported hearing him say "Today I shot in cold blood an innocent woodchuck."

C. Douglas Taylor

The *Controversy* Poems

Excerpt from a letter:

Mrs. John Rood

510 Groveland Avenue   Minneapolis, Minnesota

July 31, 1990

Dear Douglas,

To understand the [*CONTROVERSY*] verse, which is satiric, you should have a little background. Harold Mack, who started and financed the magazine, was a broker in San Francisco who was smart enough to see the 1929 crash coming and warned his partners that the market wouldn't hold. He sold out all his stock, his seat on the NY Stock Exchange, and his partnership in the brokerage company, and sat back to watch the economy collapse. He had written on economic matters and was opposed to the whole underlying system of finance which is based on debt. Money, not the bills and coins we use as small change, but money in any quantity, is simply credit, a result of book-keeping practices. The banks are government-guaranteed (note S&L crisis) but are privately owned.

A bank is allowed by law to lend (the figures may have changed somewhat but not much) ten times as much money on paper (bookkeeping) as it has in liquid cash assets. You get a loan from a bank; the bank enters a credit of the amount on its books, and you can draw on it, but pay interest until you are able to repay the loan. Harold was an advocate of having the banking business run by the government and wanted a system called "Social Credit" – a program advocated by an economist, Major Douglas, the man for whom you, my lad, were christened (together with my father's name, Charles). Money, now as then, is a matter of bookkeeping.

Back in 1935, the USA was on the gold standard, and you'll find at least one verse devoted to that. I don't suppose you know much about Huey Long*, governor of Louisiana, a real demagogue, whom I make fun of in one piece. Dear me! The whole first lot were written at Kirby, Oregon, while I was at the farm with Tom and Helen, aged 3 and 4, before you were born. The rest were done at Menlo Park, after your father brought us back to California.

Embrace your lovely wife for me. It should be no hardship.

Much love to you both,

Mother

---

* She may have forgotten, or not known how well I would know about Huey Long, having taught in one of the Louisiana state colleges thirty-some years after Long, whose influence was still quite strong; having read *All the King's Men*, which Robert Penn Warren based on the life of Long; and having had direct and indirect contact with several of the Vanderbilt "Fugitives," all of whom were friends of Warren. *CDT*

Controversy Poems

Controversy

January 1, 1935

Poems by "K K"

Rhyme With A Reason

The farmer walks behind his plow
With steady step and streaming brow.
From dawn to dark the land he tills
On level plains or rolling hills.

Behind the harrow now he plods,
Then turns again to break the clods,
And then he disks and then he drills
Till all the rows with seed he fills.

And now he sits and prays for rain
And sees with pride the growing grain,
And hopes that it may someday feed
All the hungry folk who need.

The government then sends its scholars
Who pay the oaf a thousand dollars
(For they know best, though he may wonder)
To go and plow the stuff back under.

* * * *

When Adam fell from Paradise
The dire curse was spoke
"Lo you must sweat for what you get
And bow you to the yoke."

Yet Adam's sons and their sons' sons
Were wily then as now.
For all their pains, they used their brains
And made themselves a plow.

Kressmann Taylor

And every time a man was born
Who'd rather sit than lean,
He used his head and won his bread
By making a machine.

Today a thousand hands of steel
Replace a million men.
The curse is broke, we've dropped the yoke
And man is free again.

Yes, man is free, for the machines
Can neither sweat nor tire.
They make enough of all the stuff
That mankind can desire.

Alack for pains and human brains!
There's still a curse must lurk.
We can't get beans from our machines,
They throw us out of work.

* * * *

See the sturdy CCC
Working with a pick is he;
For by work's the only way
That a man should make his pay,
(One round dollar once a day).
Yet bankers make a million dollars
With a pen and no one hollers.

* * * *

"Oh make the most of what you yet may spend!"
Old Omar, he was wise, but in the end
Just how to spend the dough you haven't got
Has puzzled older heads than mine a lot.

We'd like to fight depressions to the finish
But we haven't any credit to diminish.
"To make the most of what there is to buy"
Might be a motto for a brain trust guy.

* * *

Controversy Poems

January 15, 1935

New Deal Rhapsodies
by K. K.

It's sad – or else it may be funny
The government has got no money
But has to go down on its knees
And ask the bankers for it, please.

Yet it was not so long ago
The shoe was on the other toe,
For when the bankers felt the lash
Of all the folks demanding cash,
They hadn't a real dime in ten
Of what they owed to other men,
And lest the fierce demand should cave them
Yelled to the government to save them,
The government, that's you and you
And you, old fellow, and me too.

The government began to hum
And had a moratorium,
And told the folks the banks were dandy.
Oh yes, the government was handy.
We even loaned the banks a lot
Of dough to get them off the spot.

But now the bankers' lives are sunny
The government has need of money
And has to go down on its knees
And ask the bankers for it, please.

* * * *

Kressmann Taylor

While with brains our government
Is infinitely blest,
The mighty mental implement
Of Wallace is the best!

What reasoning powers that can surmount
This hefty mental hummock:
"Each pig unborn that takes the count
Fills an empty stomach!"

* * * *

Oh what more fully can afford
The AAA elation
Than to regard the porcupine horde
And their regeneration!

When forth the order went to cut
The porkers' population,
Our pigs were living in a rut
Of sordid propagation.

Undreamed, the sweet, serener lives
That celibacy brings,
And all they knew was to be wives,
Nor hoped for higher things.

They could not sit and contemplate
(Though pigs are sturdy sitters)
The thoughts that soar to heaven's gate.
All they had was litters.

So if we cannot now afford
Either ham or bacon,
Still we are in full accord
With the way they've taken.

We know we have done something big
For the morals of the pig.

* * * *

Controversy Poems

When history completes these pages
And rolls our story down the ages,
I fear that our posterity
Will not regard us with much glee,
For while we're curing present ills
Posterity will pay the bills.
(It's true we we haven't cured them yet,
But whoops! how we can get in debt!)
And when we're through with all our playing
Our children's kids will still be paying
A tax on food and heat and light
And getting into bed at night;
A tax on colds, a tax on jails,
And folks who bite their fingernails;
And while they're paying through the nose
They'll curse the authors of their woes.
Of course for us it might be worse,
We shan't be here to hear the curse.
Although their sorrows may impeach us,
We'll be dead and they can't reach us.
Yet somehow the suspicion mounts
That it's posterity that counts.

* * * *

Let us write a little ode
To the makers of the code,
Showing the tired business man
How to profit, with a Plan
All he has to do is swallow
And prosperity will follow.

Let us watch the lucky wight
Sitting up till late at night,
Conning rules that he next day
Will have to promise to obey.

Now alack for hopeful fools!
First he has to FIND the rules.
Most of them are hid away
In the files of NRA,
Never saw the light of day.

Let him not be discontent.
All for his own good is meant.
If the rules he cannot find
They will bring them to his mind.

The law unknown is no excuse
For its ignorant abuse;
So if he studies, or if not,
Soon in jail he'll have to rot.

* * * *

Controversy Poems

February 1, 1935

Jingles with a Joker

by K. K.

Consider the folks who have nothing to eat,
No coat on the back and no socks on the feet.
From out of his largess, hear Uncle Sam speak:
"Here's a dollar and twenty-six cents for the week."

Of course on such bounty they cannot grow fat,
But the thing isn't even as simple as that
Before they can put a thin dime in the vest
We make them submit to the destitute's test.

"Your daddy and mother, have they got a cent?"
And "What have you done with the money you've spent?"
"Ten cents for tobacco? Such luxury's out.
"And if you are hungry, how come you're still stout?

"It's forty above; do you have to have fire?"
And "What's in your cupboard? And are you a liar?"
For that is the way to ennoble the soul,
And keep them from loafing around on the dole.

* *

Like Ali Baba's brother,
When penned up in a cave,
The government is trying words
To make the door behave.

But "Open not to cotton!"
Does not effect the door,
Nor "Open higher prices!"
Nor "The regulated store!"

And though they thunder "Public works!"
"Rebuild your house with bricks!"
The magic door to plenty
Is shut, and shut it sticks.

In vain we watch them whoop it up.
They do not set us free,
Though a little word like "money"
Is the "Open Sesame!"

  * *

When the bankers start to lend
Then we'll all begin to spend.
Let us borrow on the bet
That it will get us out of debt.
That's the ticket! That's the way
To prosperity and pay.

When the bankers start to call
In again our little all,
All the money that we've spent
Plus their six and eight per cent
And the panic starts again
Shall we be the wiser men?

Shall we? Yes, like hell we will!
We'll all starve again until
Every bauble that we own
Has been hocked to pay the loan.
Then again we'll start to borrow
For another sad tomorrow.

  * * *

Oh work's the thing we need today,
The President declares.
It may be work for little pay,
But where's the man who cares?

For work's a blessing sweet and sound,
It elevates us so.
Oh what can make our lives profound,
Our better natures grow,
Like digging ditches in the ground
Or grubbing with a hoe?

Controversy Poems

This means of course (we must infer)
The man who lives in town,
For farmers' labors now incur
A governmental frown,
And lest their better natures stir
We'll pay them to lie down.

*   *

Marvel at the NRA;
Lo how subtle is its way!
Mark how from their chains it frees
The men who grow the walnut trees.

If his crop the walnut grower
Sells unto the local store
The meats must from the shells be ta'en
And neatly wrapped in cellophane.
But if to other towns he sells
He can leave them in their shells.

Kressmann Taylor

February 15, 1935

Motionless Movement in Metre

    by K. K.

Blessings on thee, little man,
Barefoot boy, whose life began
In our present panic's span.

Thought barefoot you must go
Through the rain and through the snow,
It is worth a lot to know

You've a deathless heritage
In a most resplendent age,
Filled with wealth no man can gauge.

Factories whose wheels can turn
Out everything for which you yearn,
Bread and overcoats to burn.

But for these the only tickets
Rest behind the bankers' wickets;
So for you, my lad, there's rickets.

Or anemia will do.
Both are good to harden you
For the life you must go through.

Dad and mother both will try,
They'll get a nickel, by and by.
Hush now, baby, don't you cry.

    *   *   *

Controversy Poems

Let us rejoice we have not missed
Our Saviour, the economist,
Who analyses all our grief
And speaks his solemn, sad belief
That we are in a hole because
Of deathless economic laws.

The first law that we cannot break:
The more men want, the more they'll make.
And nowadays we're making more
Than men have ever made before.

The second law we can't deny:
Although we make it, we cannot buy;
For money is a thing apart
And understanding it's an art.

And in our present case they've found
There's not enough to go around.
So they'll cut down our bread and honey,
Destroy the goods to fit the money.

They have to keep our money sound,
And since that means it can't abound
We'll all be patient and endure
That making riches makes us poor.

* * *

There was a time when youth could be
The guest of opportunity,
But now our social critics say
A "problem" is the youth today.

We'll let him train for work, but then
The jobs must go to family men.
Not only do we fail to need him,
We find it quite a chore to feed him.

We'll sigh in pity for his soul,
"It's sad that youth should lack a goal."
But on his presence we must frown
And shunt him off from town to town.

Kressmann Taylor

And when, his fibre turned to jelly,
He sticks a pistol in our belly,
In chorus we'll pofoundly chime
Of sterner ways to put down crime.

      *   *   *

We've stalked the depression
With code and with dole,
And not an impression
We've made on our goal.

But now we'll try housing
And soon you will see
We'll all be carousing
In prosperity.

Though signs without cease,
As we walk up and down,
Cry "To let" or "For lease"
Through the length of the town.

We'll borrow a billion
And at it we'll go,
And build us a million
New houses or so.

We'll wait to do penance
Till all the dough's spent,
And there still are no tenants
Who're good for the rent.

Controversy Poems

March 1, 1935

Latter Day Litany

by K. K.

Saviour of these modern days
Lord of harvest, hear us raise
Unto thee our hymn of praise.

Not for wheat in heavy sheaves,
Red fruit, glinting through the leaves,
Fatted fowl and sturdy beeves.

Not for cream within the churn,
Nor the laden honey urn
Do our votive candles burn.

But for barren fields and dry,
Corn, that 'neath a parching sky
Withered when three inches high.

In the cattle, gaunt and lean,
Dying vine and shattered bean
Thy beneficence is seen.

Thou a gracious ear hast lent
To the plans of Government
Thou hast wrought with their consent.

Lo, from east and north and south
Chants each patriotic mouth,
"Lord, we thank Thee for the drought."

# # #

Kressmann Taylor

Wallace sent his experts out
Just to scout around
And see if we were overfed,
And this is what they found:

To provide with vitamins
Each growing girl and boy,
Forty million acres more
Of land we must employ.

Cream and milk and butterfat,
Spinach, eggs and meat,
Oranges by the millions
More we ought to eat.

Now observe the government
Snapping into action,
Solving this predicament
To our satisfaction.

Forty million acres are
Removed from cultivation.
Three cheers for undernourishment!
That will save the nation.

# # #

Controversy Poems

Glory be to foreign trade!
Hope revives anew.
Greatest blessing ever made,
It will pull us through.

To the ships with shoes and clothes,
Cotton cloth and wheat;
Off with cars and radios,
Oranges and meat!

Ship them off to Timbuktu,
Ship them to Japan,
Off to China and Peru
And the Isle of Man.

Then at home in poverty
We can sit and pray
For the very goods that we
Blithely send away.

   * *

MORE POEMS

Another Eden Story

Cool on their seeking lips the apple bloom
Taught them the touch of spring together – love's lavishing
Astonished them.
Lips sped from blossom to lip. There was no more room
Between mouths for the crisp petal cup, whose vanishing
Has punished them.

Had they been children they had not been worse frightened
At that shower of crushed bloom. Fallen apart on the ground
They groped all night – what hope perhaps to have found –
Had not shaken the laden orchard and whitened
With its scatterings their heads and the dark earth around.

Caught unawares, they drew separate, unconsenting
To another season, desire for the once-seen,
Compelled
To cherish loss – the long suns dwindled for all their wanting –
Weeping, learning the timeless distance between
Hands, and the held.
Silently from their once-kiss a heavy pollen, circumventing
Death, worked in the bruised blossom. A round drop of green
The apple swelled.

But if they bite it now they will not expect sustenance.
The honey will not taste of time, but of tears
Perfectly lavished. Their tongues will remember turbulence
Sucking the death of the fruit – drinking up its impermanence
Like a benison, having let go their clutch on the years.

They will draw back their mouths
From the ceremony of death
Burned red.
Only their eyes like stilled moths
Will flutter at each breath,
Un-dead.

#   #   #

The Dancer in the World

Oh, white you shine with a blaze out of the first fire,
Eternal dancer in the world: in coursing water, and stone,
and the wild air. Listen with what bright feet
prancing upon this sullen pouch of bone,
whipping your light heel-streaks past the tremulous stars
of eyes grown sodden with what can be shown.
Joy dances near in the stone, love in the shattering street.
The making hands, the made houses tumble down
before the dancer, under the dancer's feet
crumble and ruin to powder in the defeat
and stumble of the known.
              Now, not till now will the dancer's own
White hands shape the leaping shapes of his white town
From the drubbing tumult, the crashing of break-up there,
To vault through Love, to vault through Love and Bone
To the rose and the hush of his passion, to the flowering Fire.

#   #   #

More Poems

Cock Crow

Heart upon heart like stone
    Weigheth brief.
Hurt upon hurt the bone
    Learneth fear.
Night until day the branch
    Greens the Year.

Hard upon hard, alone,
    Writhen of grief,
Not until dawn the stanch
    Know relief.
Heard then the harsh – the one
    Chanticleer.

\# \# \#

Kressmann Taylor

Bonanza in Oregon

Old Biz Nocky's hit a pocket,
　Gold's in the hills of the Siskiyous –
Hole in the ground and the nuggets chock it,
Mother lode spilled out rich to stock it.
He'll drink tonight with the logging crews.
　　What do we keep for the gold we lose?

Biz's wife is lean and weathered,
　Gold's in the hills of the Siskiyous –
Tense for the gold as a mean horse, tethered,
Dreams of her ease and a nest well feathered,
Itches for rouge and a glass to use.
　　What do we keep for the years we lose?

Biz's young ones are peaked and tattered.
　Gold's in the hills of the Siskiyous –
Eight Dollar Mountain's dews have spattered
Them trekking through brush with bare feet battered,
Sharp as coyotes and shy as ewes.
　　What do we keep for the youth we lose?

Life was drowsy and trouble lacking
　Gold's in the hills of the Siskiyous –
Spot him a three-point buck for packing
Home for meat, in a piece of sacking,
Give him his pipe and the neighbors' news.
　　What do we keep for the ease we lose?

More Poems

Biz panned Butcher Knife Creek for traces,
    __ Gold's in the hills of the Siskiyous –
Trailed the cattle, his young whitefaces,
Up where the rains give greener places.
    Yellow's the trace that the stream accrues.
What do we keep for the strength we lose?

Sank his pick with a swelling wonder,
    __ Gold's in the hills of the Siskiyous –
Rocky topsoil and glory under,
With a yell in his head like a blat of thunder,
    Knees unsteady and hands abruise!
What do we keep for the dreams we lose?

Biz went home to his wife and woke her,
    __ Gold's in the hills of the Siskiyous –
Roused the town for a night of poker,
Crowded his luck on a face-down joker.
    Hell's to pay, and the dollars ooze.
What do we keep for the hope we lose?

Old Biz Nocky's constrained to wander,
    __ Gold's in the hills of the Siskiyous –
Awake on the gravel at dawn, to ponder:
"If I turn off here it will be back yonder,"
    And, left or right, he is torn to choose.
What do we keep for the peace we lose?

# # #

Academic Ferris Wheel

Earnestly planted on the seat of erudition
Clamped in and ticketed, on an aspiring wheel
We lurch giddily skyward by stages, saluted by music,
Finding the altitude, just at first, a little daunting.

>Hey, don't get on that.
>They's no prizes.

Jolting, we are lifted above the shallow groundlings,
Who, prodded to left, to right, by bells and lights and give-
aways,
Move in activated stupor, swarming to stimuli,
The atmosphere grows cooler; we can make out the landscape.

>Come on, honey, it can't hurt you.
>Naw, le's try something else. Le's try the
>Tunnel of Love.

This is the distance we needed, the proper perspective, rarefied
Air and landscape spread out there in squares like a plotting
board.
Here we can stake out our areas; up here research and
conjecture
Promise the key to the puzzle; we'll ponder and footnote and
publish.

>Keep off it, kid. You can get stuck up there.
>Listen at that wheel squeak.

Twenty-two hundred phrases beginning with *whither* in Shakespeare
Twenty-two hundred third graders displaying an aptitude increment
Twenty-two hundred distinctions to classify culture co-ordinates
Twenty-two hundred neurotic case histories cross-tabulated
Twenty-two billion electrons doing a dance on a pin-head

>Chees, listen at that jazz!
>Whadda they think they're up to?

At this height mathematics replaces the word; we argue in tables,
Lyricise in statistics, unhampered by vague human poesies
(Old human noises of courage or laughing or weeping). We never shiver nor glance overhead toward the unclassifiable blackness.

>Ah, what's wrong? This thing appears to have stopped.
>Hold on. Keep your eyes on your lap. Don't get dizzy.

Down there somewhere cozy, under the lights and spangles
Billy hugs Daisy, and Butch has his hand inside Lindabelle's shirtfront,
Somebody hits the jackpot, and Joey grimy and wailing,
Is lost and screams for Ma. The calliope whinnies and jingles.

Kressmann Taylor

Shout louder. They can't hear us.
Ho, down there, can't you hear us?
We're up here in the dark.
How do we get down?

       #   #   #

More Poems

Roman Morning

Gino's seventeenth year broke like a rose
shaken out of the bud to flourish in bright air
one instant, before seventeen had passed
without his guessing. At first light he woke,
gathered the day into his cups of sleeves
with a thrust of arms; there prinked before the glass,
Brave Boy by Buonarroti—sculptured hair,
deep eye and questing nostril, full endowed
the full mouth, blooming, tasting where it pleased.
Kissed him a crust, trotted to church and prayed
beneath marbled skulls, where the saints' fingerbones
ache in the reliquaries—Gino unsubdued.
Six *tondi* stippled him in pigments where he preened
along centuries of statuary stone.
Straight through the *grazia plena* his purged blood
Bubbled, to bosomy benediction bent, sweet sin
encanted in an eye lift. Cockerel crowed,
plump pullet quivering downy, by mama's wing
(or aunt's) wired stiffly off. Too late, she's gone!
a flush, a rondure under the modest lace.
His gaze tastes her retreat.
        He standing slack
Within a quattrocento portico
felt the sun warm the cockles of his days
and did not lack for what he had never sprung at.
The nothing in his throat to laughter crackled.
Out in light, water splintered, and a boy sang
there in the courtyard, loading up an ass.

\# \# \#

Ornithological Garden

Treeful of eagles in the park that is
all pine and eyrie
where the wind when it comes
tosses from bough bends birds in cascading choruses:
prime Zeus gold-plume, dancing the marble boys—
the sapient owl—the hawk god needle quill—
above the sunrise water the curling ibis,
favorite of Horus—
and the black wing out of the north, the gross
raven, out of the night before name
shaped by such clumsy thumbs!
God's first try at a bird before skill
came

        before fingers feathered
        fire: struck off tanager
        and robin, that burning coal—

        from white stuff poured
        out swan and albatross,
        egret and snow goose, all

        large and luminary powers
        or in green plumed the parrot
        to nod at a green pool.

More Poems

Hear the great god-wings beating in the trees!
Under the wind-whipped trees the nursegirls
are chattering, and the children scatter
circling and crying
                                    over pavements,
over the extravagant grass,
young ones tethered by fostering,
tamed, fenced against flushing: except

that fine hair silks their skulls, flowing
out of the lion's mane, worm's floss, the billowing
air-borne plume—spun in what eddy of the wind
of aeons?
                    While the policeman coughs,
the motors gnarl, the trapped beautiful
eyes seek sideways, veer like gulls.

                #   #

Kressmann Taylor

(Untitled)

What is told is that the sin came with knowledge –
The tart juice on the teeth, the bite of dread on the heart –
But surely earlier, there had been some hint of ferment,
The whisper of "not enough" as two walked with linked fingers
Among the innocent beasts and the loud birdsong.
There was nothing intended, a thing not fated but immanent,
As blackening clouds reached out for the low sweet sun
To spread night over them before night came.

(Untitled)

When the wild goshawk screams against the summit
Of these torn mountains, and the unappeased
December air rages in sudden scatter
Of undirected strength, hail fanning the stung
Rock slab, streaking the scree of the landscape
With sweep on sweep of ice-gravel, a brother
Medium – pebble and sleet, twin eaters
Of tedium, of unbroken mountains; when the wind booms
Like drums on the boulders, whines in the canyons,
                                        a lone man
Hunches grey shoulders, his blunt back to the wind,
Old eyes patiently probing the curtains of mist,
His breath a small warm smoke in the global smoke of storm.
What is it, David, turns your rapt look upwards,
With the sheep safe in fold and the ewes broadening,
Heavy, towards lambing? What taunt to fury?
What cold prayer?

\#   \#   \#

More Poems

How Not to Write a Sonnet – a Study

A sonnet isn't hard to write or rhyme,
We talk in iambs if we talk at all;
In English that's the way the accents fall
At least a good percentage of the time.
The syllables preserve a sort of chime
As steady as the bouncing of a ball
Or footsteps moving slowly up the hall
That never pause but always seem to climb.
I've often wondered why it should be so;
You'd think a poem intricately wrought
Could stand a little freer change of pace.
Alas, these lines in marching rhythms go,
No variation for a change of thought,
Of anapest or trochee not a trace.

\# \# \#

APPENDIX

Kressmann Taylor Chronology:

August 19, 1903, born Kathrine Kressmann, Portland, Oregon
May, 1924, BA in English & Journalism, University of Oregon
June 2, 1928, married Elliott Taylor, San Francisco, California
May 27, 1930, daughter Helen Kressmann Taylor born, Redwood City, California
July 9, 1931, son Thomas Elliott Taylor born, Ross, California
March 4, 1935, son Charles Douglas Taylor born, Grant's Pass, Oregon
April, 1935, short story "Take a Carriage, Madam," published in, *Controversy* under pseudonym "Sarah B. Kennedy"
September 1938, "Address Unknown" published in *STORY* magazine
July 13, 1939, son Jonathan Golding Taylor born, Tappan, New York
1939, *ADDRESS UNKNOWN*, book, published in US by Simon & Schuster, in UK by Hamish Hamilton
1942, *UNTIL THAT DAY* published by Eagle Books
1944, *ADDRESS UNKNOWN* film, Columbia Pictures
Sept. 1947, Guest lecturer, Gettysburg College, Gettysburg, Pennsylvania
1948 – 1966, Assoc. Prof., Gettysburg College, Gettysburg, Pennsylvania
Dec. 25, 1953, Elliott Taylor died, Gettysburg, Pennsylvania
1953 - 1965, during summer vacations, wrote 10 more short stories (included in *ELEVEN STORIES and More*)
August, 1966, retired from teaching, moved to Florence, Italy
1967, *DIARY OF FLORENCE IN FLOOD* published in US by Simon & Schuster, in UK by Hamish Hamilton as *ORDEAL BY WATER*
1967, married John Rood, Minneapolis, Minnesota, and settled near San Casciano, Val de Pesa, Tuscany

June 29, 1974, John Rood died, Minneapolis, Minnesota
1978, completed novel, *STORM ON THE ROCK*, (published in France as *JOURS D'ORAGE* in 2008)
1995, *ADDRESS UNKNOWN* commemorative edition published by STORY Press.
June 2, 1995, interview, *Northern Lights & Insights*, #342, Hennepin County Library, Minnesota Public Television
1995, approved plan for first translation of *ADDRESS UNKNOWN* (into Hebrew) by Asher Tarmon, Israel
1996, Died July 14, Minneapolis, Minnesota

End Notes

(1) "The Blown Rose," published in *Woman's Day* Sept. 1953, in French *Ainsi mentent les hommes,* 2004, & in German *So Traumen die Frauen*, 2016. Dramatized on CBS Studio One, as "They Served the Muses," 1958

(2) "Take a Carriage, Madam," published under pseudonym Sarah B. Kennedy, in *Controversy*, April 1, 1935, in French *Ainsi revent les femmes*, 2006, & in German *So Traumen die Frauen*, 2016

(3) The Red Slayer," published in *Woman's Day* (February 1956), & in French *Ainsi mentent les hommes,* 2004

(4) "Passing Bell," published in *Univ. of Kansas City Review*, Autumn, 1956, in French *Ainsi revent les femmes*, 2006, & in German *So Traumen die Frauen*, 2016

(5) "Mr. Pan," published in British *Argosy,* 1961, as illustrated book in French translation as **Monsieur Pan**, 2009, by Editions Autrement/Flammarion

(6) "Goat Song"; published in *London Magazine*, 1955. Edited by author, 11/63, published in French *Ainsi revent les femmes*, 2006

(7) "Girl in a Blue Rayon Dress," published in *Woman's Day*, April 1958, in British *Argosy* (as "Girl in a Blue Dress"), in French *Ainsi revent les femmes*, 2006, & in German *So Traumen die Frauen*, 2016

(8) "The Pale Green Fishes" published in *Woman's Day* (May 1953), *Best American Short Stories of 1954*, & French *Ainsi mentent les hommes*, 2004

(9) "The Midas Tree" 1965, previously unpublished in USA. Copyright 2000, by Charles Douglas Taylor. Included in translation as "Melancolie" in French *Ainsi mentent les hommes,* 2004

(10) "First Love," published in *Woman's Day,* Nov. 1957, in British *Argosy* (as "The Grey Bird"), 1961, in French *Ainsi revent les femmes*, 2006 & in German *So Traumen die Frauen*, 2016

(11) "Michael," published in *Woman's Day,* July, 1959. Copyright 1959, by Kathrine Kressmann Taylor

OTHER WORKS

By KATHRINE KRESSMANN TAYLOR:

"Address Unknown," *STORY* Magazine, September, 1938

ADDRESS UNKNOWN, Simon and Schuster, 1939, CreateSpace 2015, Amazon/Kindle 2016

UNTIL THAT DAY, 1942 / annotated and reissued as *DAY OF NO RETURN, 2003*

DIARY OF FLORENCE IN FLOOD (ORDEAL BY WATER) 1967

AINSI REVENT LES FEMMES, Editions Autrement, 2006

AINSI MENTENT LES HOMMES, Editions Autrement, 2006

MONSIEUR PAN, Editions Autrement, 2006

JOURS D'ORAGE, Flamarrion, 2008

By C. Douglas Taylor:

HOW TO PILOT AN AEROPLANE, (1973, 1974, 1978; 1986) *General Aviation Press*

ARTIFICIAL TURF, (2003), *Xlibris,* e-book (2017)

DOWNTOWN DUCKS, (2003), *Xlibris,* by Douglas & Catherine Taylor;

THE REACTOR, (2008), *Create Space,* e-book

THANKSGIVING, (2012), *Create Space,* by Douglas & Catherine Taylor,

POETRY AND ART, (2015) *Create Space,* by Catherine & Douglas Taylor.

Printed in Great Britain
by Amazon

Eleven of the best stories by best-selling author Kathrine Kressmann Taylor (Address Unknown), ten previously published in major English and American periodicals; one selected for Best American Short Stories of 1954; another that was published separately in French translation, and another that was dramatized on television (Westinghouse Studio One) in the 1950s.

Also a collection of her finest poetry, including some satiric political verse published in Controversy magazine in the 1930s.

With a 2016 Introduction and notes by the author's son, author/poet C. Douglas Taylor.

ISBN 9781534647978